Murder at

CW00670392

The Enchanted Mill Series, Book 1

By

C. E. Davis

www.publishnation.co.uk

Cast of characters

- Cathy Collins genealogist, with an online crystal store
- Fluffy / Oskar the scruffy ginger tom familiar
- Sally Buckley
- Uncle John Collins
- Aunt Audrey Jones
- Uncle Charles Jones
- Cousin Elizabeth Jones
- Solicitor Roger Davies
- Mill Owner Harold Butterworth
- Ex-husband Martin Bradbury/ Bradshaw/Bradgate
- Gillian Bradshaw, The second wife
- June and Kenneth Collins (Parents deceased)

The Coven members

- Wendy Smithies
- Kim Smithies
- Roger Davies
- Harold Butterworth
- Margaret Gartside
- Edith Stanworth
- Betty Barratt
- Desdemona Jones
- Mary Mellor
- Pat Armstrong

- Regina Carrington (Reggie)
- Cynthia Hobbs
- Cathy Collins – making the 13 members of the Coven.

Mill Ghost

- Clara Jane Holroyd
- John and Betty Holroyd
- The four bullies – George Bob Tommy Fred
- Pearl and Ruby -Mill ghosts (sisters)

Others

- Brian and Adam - The Detective Magic Police Agency
- Stephen and Hamish the blind cat / familiar
- Alphin and Alderman- Security /Shapeshifting Giants
- Rimmon and Rowan, sisters, and water nymph
- Peter and his wife Susie - the County Archaeologist
- David and Nigel archaeologists, who are brothers.
- Gilbert Butterworth- the owner the old workhouse (Harold's cousin)
- Donna Maria – Desdemona's missing granddaughter
- Rebecca – Pat's granddaughter
- Inese – Regina's granddaughter

Chapter 1

The Solicitors

Cathy was at the solicitors, in Green Valley, for the reading of her grandmothers will. She had not really known either of her grandmothers, but this one was on her maternal grandmother. Her mother June, and father, Kenneth Collins, had left the area when Cathy was an infant. Visits to the area, had been rare. When she had received the letter about the reading of the will, she did not even know that her Grandma Sally had died. So, she had in fact, missed her own grandmother's funeral.

Cathy's own parents had been tragically killed in a skiing accident when she was a toddler and she had been raised by her father's brother. Uncle John Collins. He was a quiet man, a confirmed bachelor, lacking some emotional skills, but he had taken in the orphan toddler and raised her in his own way – fed, watered, and educated. Cathy left her Uncle John to go off to university. Where she met and married her ex-husband whilst only twenty-two. Cathy thought back to her own parents and realised that Sally would now be with them in the family vault - she must go back and visit soon.

Cathy was as surprised to be sat around the table, as were the other people sat there. After introductions she realised, she had an elderly aunt and uncle and a much older cousin. They did not seem that pleased to see her.

Cathy sat and daydreamed about her inheritance. What would she receive – money, a ring? Or more likely a duck ornament or such like. Eventually the very stuffy solicitor coughed and brought her attention back into the room. "Catherine, your grandmother has bequest to you, her lock up storage unit at the local business centre. The goods left inside are yours to do as you will with. If you decide to retain the unit then the rent has been paid for the next couple of years, so that should not be a financial worry to you."

The other three people in the room sniggered between themselves. "Less for us to deal with," murmured the elderly Aunt.

Cathy sat and listened to the rest of the reading of the will. She did not know these people and they certainly had not helped with her upbringing after her parents died. One of them must be her mother's sibling – but which one? Uncle John her father's brother had brought her parents bodies back from Switzerland after the skiing accident and arranged the funeral. In fact, Cathy could not recall these three people or of having ever met them in her life. The cousin had been bequeathed the tiny house her grandmother had lived in and was already googling how much money she would receive from selling it. The aunt and uncle jointly received what bit of money there was – nothing to write home about.

She let herself daydream again about what was in the lock up storage unit – an old painting or antique she could get some cash from. Cathy was not short of money, she ran her own online business, but no one would turn down a bit extra – would they? Or maybe, it was just a trick to let her remove all the rubbish at her expense, ever optimistic Cathy thought. At least she may have somewhere to store her stock for her crystal jewellery business, as her small cottage was getting a bit cramped.

When the will had been overseen and everyone knew their share, the solicitor seems to soften and be more approachable. He handed her a parcel, which looked like a book, or a photo album? He handed her the keys to the unit and told her the location. He then added that the parcel could only be opened once she had gone inside the storage unit, and that it would all be explained then. "*How mysterious*" she thought to herself.

The obligatory cup of tea and biscuits were brought out, and Cathy had a chance to talk to the three relatives she was with. It turned out that the woman was her mothers, much older sister, Aunt Audrey and her husband, Uncle Charles and the daughter was Cousin Elizabeth. They had noses stuck that far in the air, that one could see right up the nostril. "Oh, please do keep in touch darling Catherine" her aunt stumbled to say to her, and they then left the office.

"Cathy," The solicitor called her back. "Please call me Roger. There is something I must tell you about your grandmother before you leave." Now Cathy was very confused; a family so close she never knew; a storage unit to clean up; what would she learn now?

"Your grandmother left you an unbelievably valuable part of her estate, one that few people know about. She knows that you will take things a day at a time, learning the skills necessary to follow her. If you need anything, and I mean anything, please give me a call. It will be a new and interesting journey for you, but your grandmother has every faith that you will succeed. She wanted me to tell you that she has watched you growing up and kept a keen interest in your life. Your Uncle John was not all stiff collars and cufflinks, he knew this day would arrive sometime. I cannot say any more at this time. You will need to go to the lock up unit at your earliest convenience and things will become clearer, although if I do say, stranger for you!" And with that he gave her his business card with his personal phone number and email on and showed her the door.

Cathy's cottage was near to the solicitor's office, and she had walked there. She walked back slowly to her own small cottage, her mind overflowing with all this added information she was trying to understand. A chilly wind blew past her making her shiver. She quickened her pace, looking up at the moors and hills of her beloved Green Valley. The area had been formed, from a glacier sliding through the valley, thousands of years before. The name Green Valley was so appropriate, as at this time of year everything was in bloom and so lush.

She decided a strong coffee, feet up and laptop were her best plans for the present, as it was late afternoon by the time, she reached her house.

Cathy checked her laptop and emails. Any orders for her online business could wait until morning Business was good, but the couple of orders waiting would wait for tomorrows post. She decided a long hot bath and early night would be best for her, and a clear head for tomorrow, for when she goes to check out her inheritance. Fluffy, her large scruffy ginger tomcat meowed in agreement.

Chapter 2

The Mill

Cathy did not get much sleep; her night was spent tossing and turning, and she had some very weird dreams about wizards and witches. She felt sure she had heard her grandmother tell her in her dreams that the world would be fine now, but to be aware that not all people are as they seem.

If only she was still married to Martin Bradbury; at least she would have had someone to discuss all this with, but he was on a cruise with his latest fling. That made her smile and realised if she was suddenly wealthy, that man would no longer have access to her money. It made her glad she was actually divorced. It was a shock at the time that he had married her thinking she was loaded with her Uncle John's money and her parents' insurance money, but what he hadn't known, was that the money was in trust for her own children for some reason, and that she only got a generous allowance.

This allowance had allowed her to set her up online business, and Martin was not very happy that he had to go out to work and earn his own money, hence he was on the cruise with his latest rich conquest. Although this was the second since they had divorced. If only I could show him, I was not useless. The insults he had called her made her cringe inside. It had taken a while to get over him, and she was still only twenty-eight!! Well at least he was unaware of her inheritance now and would not be in her life anymore to belittle and expect a lazy life through her!

First though, she knew she must check to see if any orders or messages for her shop "Cathy's Crystal Cave," She had always been obsessed with crystals and essential oils throughout her life. Uncle John was a geologist and had a collection of rocks at home, that was where her love of stones and nature came from. He had been kind and explained what all the rocks were, and where they were from in the world. She had started collecting at an early age. Then eventually after studying business studies herself at

4

university, Cathy decided she wanted her own independence and created her online store.

Eventually she had seen quite a success with the shop, but instead of giving the money to the idle ex, she put the profits back into the business, expanding from crystals to making crystal jewellery. When the ex-left for someone with money, Cathy held her crystal and essential oil even closer to her to help the hurt and betrayal. It was only over two years since he had left her for a rich woman from out of town. But Cathy was getting over things slowly. Not that she had replaced him, it would take a long time to regain the trust of someone new. She wanted someone to love her, not the thought of the money she was linked to. They had sold their house they had bought together, and so she rented a small cottage, which came with Fluffy the cat already installed. She had not minded the cat, as it was very friendly, and she felt he protected her already.

After, finally checking the orders, messages and getting showered and dressed, she thought she had better go and check out the mysterious lock up. Fluffy the cat tried to get into her bag to go with her. "What are you doing you daft cat, I won't be long." He looked up at her with his huge eyes, but he was to stay at home.

Cathy knew the area well and the old textile mill was near the large lake she used to go walking around, not that she had ever been to the mill itself. She drove across the old rickety bridge, and saw the heron stood in the river, waiting for its lunch. She parked in the car park with the sign "Visitors to the mill only." She smiled to herself and thought that a lot of people would park here to go walking around the area. A river flowed by the car park and the old mill pond was further around on the old mill rough road, towards the back of the building, The mill itself was an imposing building; parts of it were built back in the 1850's and had been built on many times since. She would have to do some research into this place; it was amazing. Walking up the mill drive, and following the reception signs, Cathy saw a row of old workers cottages; twelve small terraced and two larger houses, which she assumed would have been the manager's houses. The imposing office block came in front of her, she

5

thought to herself; it would make a fabulous living accommodation.

Cathy hesitated. She had no idea where she would find the lockup that was now hers, it was unit 3. She knew she would have to go into the reception to ask. She did not know why she felt so hesitant though. Going through the huge white doors she arrived back in time; the reception area was still in 1920s décor, with mahogany-boarded panelling on the walls with three doors off it and a huge staircase leading upstairs.

One of the doors had a sign for the reception so she opened it and found herself at a small counter and rang the bell for attention. She need not have bothered, as all eyes in the room where on her, which made her feel even more uncomfortable. It was as though they all knew who she was, yet she knew none of them. A young girl came over and asked if she could help Cathy. "Oh yes please she said, I am looking for unit 3 and have no idea where to go." At that moment, a door opened, and a very distinguished older gentleman walked in, and the office staff all looked down at the computer keyboards as if they had been caught cheating.

"Welcome Catherine, I am Harold, the owner of this fabulous building. The ladies should have told me that you had arrived. Follow me this way please." He led her into the room he had come from. What an amazing room; the board room had a huge table down the middle and walled panelling like the entrance hall, but the atmosphere in it felt out of this world.

"Take a seat Catherine, I need to explain a few things to you." Harold said to her. "My name, as I have said is Harold. I was a close friend of your grandma Sally. I will show you to her unit myself. The mill is not like other buildings in the area, some parts are off limits to many people. As you get used to the mill itself, I will show you around and explain where you can and cannot go, but to start with, the cellars are totally restricted to a few members of staff only.

Your grandmother was one of our first tenants when we turned the textile mill into the business centre. The top story of the mill is now apartments. Quite a few of the tenants are reclusive, so you may not come across them. The ground floor and first floor are made up of small business and storage units.

Your grandmother's unit is at the other end of the building, one of the, shall we say, exceptional units. I think it will be better to chat once we get inside Sally's unit".

With that, Harold stood up and they left the board room through a door that led back to the entrance hall. Harold led the way down a rabbit warren of small units. She smiled to herself as she imagined all the people behind the closed doors working away, or whatever they were doing. She could hear the odd radio blaring from some units. Harold walked with her, talking about why the textile mill had stopped production and the history of then being turned into storage units and small workspaces. The mill had been built next to the Dove Stone River and was a woollen mill to start with, and then changing to a cotton mill in the 1940s. The main customers had been tyre manufacturers in the midlands, until 2001, when the mill ceased production, as the Chinese import market made things difficult. Then the business centre had been created.

Cathy felt that he was quite excited to be taking her himself to the mysterious lock up. She looked over at Harold and was surprised he only looked to be in his mid-sixties, yet her grandmother had been in her late eighties when she passed away. There was something in the water that flowed by the mill. She could not help wondering why her grandmother's unit was so different that she had a personal showing by the mill owner. She was beginning to feel excited to be finding out, she just hoped she would not be disappointed and find herself lots of work that she did not really need. She clutched the parcel the solicitor had given to her, and her mind wondered to what was in it. She did hope it was a photograph album or family tree, something to show her ancestry.

They had reached the end of a long corridor, lit by fluorescent lights, no windows, just doors to the units. In front was a fire door, with a sign for Emergency use only. Harold opened this door and at the side you could see a smaller door, which was almost hidden away from them, and in front the emergency exit to the main car park outside. Harold took the keys from Cathy and unlocked the hidden door. This opened into a bright corridor; not much in the corridor, just a long white tunnel that seemed to lead to nowhere. They eventually stopped outside of another semi

7

hidden door. Cathy felt a rush of chilly air swish through her; she had felt something like that in her dreams last night too.

Harold paused; he seemed lost for words. "Err," he mumbled to himself rather than to Cathy, "you didn't know much about your grandmother, did you?"

Cathy shook her head. "Why, is there a problem with the inheritance and the contents of the storage space? I had hoped to get it emptied and sorted out as soon as I could if, I am honest."

"Right," hesitantly Harold then saw she was carrying the parcel from the solicitor. "Let's get this started, get inside and put the kettle on and have a cuppa." Cathy was surprised that this unit would have a kettle, let alone a cuppa.

Harold opened the door, and the light came on automatically, Cathy could tell immediately that this was no ordinary lock up storage space, as in front of her was the most impressive lounge and apartment she had ever seen. She went through a small vestibule into a fabulously decorated lounge, grey leather suite, pale grey floor tiles, even a large TV on the wall. The floor felt warm, and Harold smiled and explained that there was underfloor heating installed. He told Cathy to take a seat, whilst he went to make the coffee. Before she had time to take in her surroundings, he was back with a tray full of coffee and goodies. "That was quick." She smiled.

"Let us begin, I think we should start from the beginning. Hold tight, Cathy, your grandmother was a practising witch. In fact, she was from a long ancestry of witches. She was the longest serving member of our Coven, yes Coven. We have male and female witches, although the men are sometimes known as Wizards. Both your solicitor and I belong to this Coven, and we are here to help protect and guide you through the process of you learning the role to take over from Sally, your grandmother. This apartment is where she spent most of her time. The cottage in the village, was the outward appearance of the wonderful person your grandmother was, not everyone in the family believes in witchcraft. The house is of little value, compared to this apartment, and that is why it was left in the inheritance to Elizabeth, your estranged cousin. That side of your family know nothing of this side of Sally."

8

Cathy sat, speechless, she had just been called a witch, by a wizard? What trick were these people playing on her?

Harold sensing her unease, motioned to the parcel next to Cathy on the sofa. "The parcel you have brought with you, it is time to open it and see the contents, Harold motioned to the bundle next to her. Cathy pulled the plastic bag towards her, concern across her face as to what this was going to reveal. Her hopes were that it could be the photo album, but now she had no idea at all. She pulled out the contents and was relieved to find it was a book, although it felt an incredibly old book. "GRIMOIRE OF THE BUCKLEY FAMILY."

"Could you tell me what a grimoire is please?" she asked, looking at the book that she held, the pages looked to be blank. Harold was fully composed now, he had even relaxed, now the big secret had been revealed. "There is a letter in the front of the grimoire from your grandmother, please read it and it will explain a little more to you. Cathy found the letter, which appeared to be on an old piece of parchment, in the most fabulous calligraphy handwriting.

My Dearest Catherine

I know that this will be one enormous shock for you to comprehend fully, but as you know, your parents took you away from this area when you were incredibly young, you descend from an exceptionally extensive line of witches. Your parents were concerned when you were young that even as a small child you showed that you would be an exceptional witch as you grew older. The idea was to keep you away from the Coven to be trained by your mother and myself, so no bad influences could get to you. Your mother was a kitchen witch, a witch that could create the most wonderful cookery skills. Your father was or appeared to be a normal human, but there was history in his family too. It was after a lot of collaboration with both the families, that you left the area, and very rarely came back. When your parents were so tragically killed in the skiing accident, I did ask for custody of you, but your father had left strict instructions in his will for your Uncle John to be your guardian. I wish I had been around you more to help you develop in the way you should have with your witchcraft and to be able to introduce you personally to this fabulous, enchanted mill.

9

When knowing my mortal time on this planet was ending, I set the steps in place for you to take over from me, in my place in the Coven. I know you will be shocked, surprised and even maybe speechless. But this is not a joke, this is going to be a wonderful, if steep learning curve.

Uncle John always stayed connected with me regarding your progress, I was thrilled to hear about your love for crystals, you already have a bit of being a crystal witch in you. (He also told me about your wretched ex-husband, my word, he will be laughing on the other side of his face if he knew what your future has in store.)

The next step for you now is to make yourself at home here, I hope the fixtures and decorations is to your liking. There is no rent here, as the Coven owns the actual mill. You must explore the mill too, but until you have found your bearings, please let Harold show you round. The cottage you live in, in the human world, is now in your name, yes, I was your property owner. That will be your "Real world" and here is the witch world.

Finally, please give Oskar (Or Fluffy) as you call him some salmon and an extra cuddle or two, he himself will explain!

Sit back, study the grimoire of your family, it dates back hundreds of years. A lot of the pages will appear blank to start with, they will come to you when you are ready. Use the apartment as your own, as it is now.

I will be around, keeping an eye on you, most ghosts are friendly, I can assure you.

Your loving grandmother
Sally Buckley x

Harold smiled as he watched her take in the contents of the letter. This young woman had just learnt she had inherited a luxury apartment, a secret life and was a witch too. A shock for anyone to take in.

"I will let you get settled in," he told Cathy, "Take time to explore the apartment. Through there is a workshop, with a door that leads out towards the car park rather than going through the mill. I will let all this information sink in, but I will be around, as my apartment is the opposite side of the fire exit! As I said before, please before exploring the mill, let me show you around, as some of the tenants do not know you are here yet, I would like to do the introductions." He gave her his business card with his mobile and email on so she could call him. "I will call back across later, so good to finally meet you Cathy, if you are half as kind and intelligent as your grandmother, you will be amazing. Do not worry about the magic, Roger and I are your guardians and will point you the right direction to follow,"

With that he left the apartment and Cathy surveyed her surroundings. Time to explore she thought, this was hers now and all that came with it. The lounge led through to a fabulous kitchen with dark grey units against the white walls, it even had a kitchen island in the centre, Cathy thought the kitchen alone was bigger than the downstairs of her own cottage. The bathroom was the same, small spotlights on the ceiling and walk in shower and a bathtub. There were even two bedrooms, she wondered if the person that had created these rooms had been watching her, as it was everything she had ever wanted in a property.

Then through another door was the shop space. A workshop like the one she has at her own cottage - practically identical, but larger, with display cabinets, already stocked with the most wonderful jewellery. A desk with a fancy computer system was already displaying the website for "Cathy's Crystal Cave." She sat at the stool behind the counter and could not believe her eyes. This place was incredible, she could run her online business from here straight away, or even from both home and the mill.

She could not quite take in all that had happened. But my she knew that her grandmother had loved her all these years and left her something so special. Again, she felt the cold breeze swish by her, was that her grandma she thought, every time she had thought of her, she had experienced a cold breeze near her??

As Cathy turned to go back into the small corridor to the apartment, she noticed a tiny door hidden in the wall. She reached for her bundle of keys and tried each one, none of them worked, so she thought that must just lead back to the mill itself. *"Time for another coffee"* she thought, *"a strong one now, and I suppose I need to have a look at the grimoire book"*.

It was only early afternoon, and she had no one to answer to. She had called her Uncle John the previous evening and told him about her inheritance. He had told her to ring him again, when

11

she had learnt what was in the unit. She now wondered if he already knew a lot more than he ever let on. After all her grandmother's letter had said that he had been in touch with her grandmother.

Cathy went into the kitchen to see what if anything was in the fridge. To her amazement the fridge and cupboards were filled with all her favourite items. Even the coffee maker was the same as her model at home and the coffee pods the ones she adored. She said aloud, to herself, "coffee please" and before she could turn around the coffee pot was making brewing her coffee. Now that is magic, she said to herself again.

She took her coffee back into the lounge, noting there were not many windows, but it did not feel dark. Outside the mill had looked imposing, dark, and grimy from the years of service. But this room was the opposite, light, airy, warm, and amazingly comfortable. Kicking off her trainers she curled up on the sofa, she took the grimoire out of the package and felt a sudden warmth flow through her fingers and through her body.

Nothing was surprising anymore, this felt like the family magic was already seeping back into her body and awakening the powerful energy, that she must have always had buried deep in her soul. She had never thought about witches or wizards, only in fantasy films and novels, yet today she had been in the company of two wizards and found out she was the descendant of an extensive line of witches. Scary or what she thought to herself. She turned the pages of the grimoire; some blank and others came to life with words or old fashioned emojis. She turned each page as she read and tried to understand all that was happening.

Chapter 3

Fluffy aka Oskar

Cathy woke suddenly; she felt strange and did not know where she was for a few moments, she remembered going to sleep on the sofa of her late grandmother's apartment. But now, she had a blanket over her, and something was clawing at her. She sat up and saw that Fluffy was in the blanket with her, fast asleep.

That seemed odd, "Hey, Fluffs how on earth did you get in here?" The scruffy large ginger tom stretched as he looked her in the eye. "You can call me Oskar in here," he smiled as though he had got the cream of the milk. "I am your familiar, as I was your grandmothers."

Now Cathy thought she was dreaming, a talking cat, which had somehow got from her small cottage to this place. "What on earth is happening to me" she answered to her grinning cat.

"Let me explain, all witches have a familiar, not always a cat, it can be any creature. Although cats are always the best at familiars. Your grandmother left me with the apartment, especially to keep an eye on you and report back. No, I was not spying on you, if you need to ask. I must say though, it is so good to be able to talk again to you know you, now that you know your history and duty to the Coven. I will be able to help with your lessons on the magic learning, and you can now run your crystal business from here and have more room in that tiny human house. By the way, I heard the letter from Sally saying I like salmon and extra cuddles – please no more of that tinned rubbish, yuk."

Cathy shook herself to make sure she was not dreaming. Somehow, she whisked up another coffee - which Oskar aka Fluffy was impressed with. "I knew you had magic in you. Now we need to start with the grimoire, at page one. I know you have had a look through the book, but now the lessons."

The Grimoire gave a little shake, disturbing Cathy from her thoughts. "*Crickey, how spooky*" she thought to herself, but slowly reached her arm out to lift the grimoire. As she flicked through the pages, she could still see a lot of blank pages.

Let us start at the beginning, she told herself, *'The Grimoire of the Buckley Family, Green Valley, began by Tabitha Buckley, in 1624'.*

"Wow 1624, my goodness that's centuries ago, and now in my possession." Turning to the frontispiece of the grimoire, Cathy found her family tree, which included her name at the bottom of it. With her mother, June and then her Grandmother Sally. She immersed herself into the people going back on the tree, there were around fifteen women's names, she guessed it averaged around four a century.

Generations of witches, how had she never known this before. She continued looking through the large book on her knee, totally lost in her thoughts. Fluffy/ Oskar sat beside her, just like his usual position at her own house, yet now he could talk; was she still dreaming. Cathy had always thought she knew her family history, and had finished many family trees for her friends, but nothing prepared her for this line of grandmothers; all of them apparently magical.

She decided she could use another mug of coffee, to keep her going. So, she thought hard and clicked her fingers. As she got up to go through to the kitchen, suddenly a perfect looking mug of coffee was on the table in front of her. Was it the deep thoughts, or the clicking of the fingers she wondered?

Life was taking on a strange turn, since she went to the solicitor's office yesterday. Cathy thought she had known about her ancestry, and the fall out that made her parents leave. Now everything was getting turned upside down. For goodness's sake, she could conjure a coffee by clicking her fingers (or by deep thought – or both).

Cathy drank her magic coffee, as she continued looking through the grimoire. She felt the warmth spread through her as she held it. "*Was that the magic?*" she smiled to herself. As she went from page to page, the writing appeared before her. Words that were aimed directly for Cathy to read. She felt like she was having a déjà vu moment, as she read the ancestor details and in particular about her grandma Sally.

14

Yet again she felt the cold shiver go through her. At the same time Fluffy aka Oskar began to purr extremely loud. "Do you know something I don't?" She surprised herself by talking to the cat.

"Can you feel it too?" he smiled, "you do know what it is when you feel the cold wind around you?"

"I have no idea; I just keep feeling a cold shiver now and again. More so when I talk or think about my grandmother, and in this apartment."

"It is Sally, she is letting us know she is with us," Fluffy aka Oskar cried. "When she died, she did not pass over, she stayed behind to help you achieve your full potential, once she is strong enough, we will be able to see her. Her ghost will be like human to us, and those that can see ghosts. Obviously only a select few."

"Her ghost, we will be able to see my grandma as if she were alive? I have never seen a ghost, I do not really believe that they can exist, well until now that is. Oh, my what a day this is turning out to be, getting more unnerving by the minute," Cathy's stomach was turning, and she found herself trembling.

"Calm down, deep breaths" the cat instructed her, "Cathy, it will all be ok, this is what you have been destined for all your life. You will not be alone, there are plenty of people out there looking after us. You will be surprised with who is a witch, or a wizard, or paranormal. Now back to the grimoire and read, then in the next few days you will be ready for your lessons. I want to get back into the Temple room, and for that I need you to be ready. Have a sniff of that oil you carry with you, that will stop you feeling anxious."

Very confused, and taking out her favourite oil blend, she rolled it on her temples and took a deep breath. Cathy replied to Fluffy aka Oskar, "we can go into the workshop already."

"Not your shop, the workspace behind the apartment, it is called the Temple Room, you have not been in yet, you will not be able to open the door yet, yes you tried all the keys, but it will not let you in until the time the magic thinks you are ready."

Cathy realised he was talking about the small door in the corridor between the apartment and the shop, "what is behind that door?" Curiosity got the better of her. But as in the old-fashioned saying, curiosity did not kill the cat. He just replied, "read the grimoire, learn the words it is telling you, otherwise we will be having to go back to the human house, as it is now getting late."

Cathy looked at her watch and did not realise what time it was, but she knew she needed to read on. She had another hour or so before she needed to go back to her own house, but why rush when she had everything she needed here. Although, she did not feel ready to spend the night in this old, enchanted mill and her grandmother's shivery ghost in this apartment, not just yet!

Cathy continued with learning the grimoire, which was now hers. It felt as if parts of herself were reawakening from a very deep sleep, as she read about the precious witches in her family. The power, that she was slowly believing, would be hers soon. She came across a reference to the Temple room, "shall we try again Fluffy aka Oskar," she called out, as he seemed to have gone exploring himself. "Please do, I will lead the way," as he appeared from nowhere.

They walked quickly towards the shop at the end of the apartment, down the short corridor and stood next to the small, very unnoticeable door. Cathy noticed that the cold breeze was with them, and she thought she heard a voice saying, "*try the handle.*"

"Which key is it?" she said aloud and both the voice in her head and Fluffy aka Oskar replied, "the handle – no key for this door is required."

Cautiously Cathy stepped forward and held the ornate door handle. She felt the same warm sensation has when she held the grimoire. "Door, tell me how I open you? she murmured to herself, more than anyone else, but nothing happened. "Hold the handle, feel the magic, set the intent, hold and feel, that's how it is done," the voice said to her, she thought it must be her grandmother or her ancestors teaching her.

Still nothing happened, she held the handle, felt the magic flow through her. She was disappointed, the day had been full of new things, but obviously not ready just yet. With a final go, Cathy thought she heard the door click, but nothing moved,

"The time is not right yet, a little more reading, and then the door will open, and you will be ready for your real lessons. Go back to your cottage now, rest and come back tomorrow and we will try again" The voice told her.

16

"Grandma, is that you talking in my head? Are you with us Grandma" Cathy whispered,

"Yes child, I am with you and dear old Oskar. Now get some sleep, tomorrow will be a long day," her grandma replied.

"Come along Oskar, as I can't keep calling you Fluffy aka Oskar, let's call it a day and get home, we have orders to process." She felt defeated and deflated. She had learnt so much in one day but knew this was just the beginning.

Cathy and Oskar left the mill, via the shop front door. She thought it would be easier than trying to find her way through the mill on her own. Arriving back at her own small cottage Cathy looked around and tried to comprehend what had happened. She was a witch herself, but with a lot of learning ahead of her.

To get back to normal. She checked the orders on her laptop, surprising herself how many orders were waiting. *"How long had she been away?"* – not that long. She checked her website and saw that there had been updates and the site looked impressive – even magic had hit her sales. She processed the orders, answered any queries, and finally had a soak in her own bathtub and cooked her own food. Climbing into bed she wondered what would happen next in this new mysterious life she had now got. Yet, she knew deep down, she was not afraid of what was ahead. Oskar snuggled next to her and soon both were in a deep sleep.

Chapter 4

The Temple Room

Cathy's life turned in to a regular pattern, mornings at home doing her work; as a normal person does. In the afternoons she would drive herself and Oskar to the mill and practice her magic. Read the grimoire and learn as much as she could. She was also getting the shop ready to be able to move her own stock (alongside the stock her grandma had set up for her); so that she could work from the mill shop, instead of home.

She was getting more practice, in the magic of making a coffee and food. Harold had shown her some more spells and shown her around the huge mill. She still felt the chilly air swirl around her, which was knew was her grandma. She felt it was time to try the door again. "I can do this" she told herself, over and over.

Cathy and Oskar went to the door, the small wooden door down the corridor to the shop. Cathy held the handle and took a deep breath. "I CAN do this." Cathy felt the warmth flood through her arms again, the handle became warm to touch, slowly the handle turned slightly, and the door began to open – on its own. Cathy was too surprised to do anything. Oskar ran into the room – running round and round. Whilst Cathy was overly cautious. Taking in every inch of this secret room.

She had never seen anything like it, the room was not a tiny cupboard under the stairs, as she had thought it was it was amazing. It must have been the same size as the whole apartment. The walls were a mixture of purples and lilacs, with a tough of cream. Although there was no natural lighting, the room felt very well-lit with a subdued lighting that enhanced the whole room.

Oskar was busy chasing around and trying to show Cathy everything at once. Cathy found the light switch, which was a dimmer switch, so she turned the light brighter; enabling her to see the room more clearly. It was an outstanding room, with workbenches the same as those in the shop, but much bigger. At the far end of the room, Cathy saw what looked like an altar. As she made her way to that end of the room, she felt the rush of chilly air wrap around her. It was indeed a Temple Room.

"Grandma, are you with me? how do I get to see you?" Cathy had lost all hesitation of seeing the ghost of her grandma, the excitement of the last few weeks had surpassed any nerves that she had, now that she was in this room, she knew she was ready.

"The Grimoire, place it on the altar," Cathy heard the voice of her grandma, not so much as in her head, but aloud. She ran back into the lounge and grabbed the heavy book. She put the large heavy book on the altar, there appeared to be a place especially for the book. A breeze flew past her, and she saw the grimoire open itself, (or was it her grandmother was opening it?)

"Concentrate on your grandmother," the voice told her, "Place your hands upon the open pages and feel the warmth." Oskar took his place next to Cathy, looking up at her and nodding, "The time is right, you are ready, the room would not let you in if you were not capable. I know it seems amazingly fast, how all your life has changed, but please, proceed. You need to set the 'Intent or intentions' ask; what it is you are searching for."

Cathy took the small steps to the altar, the candles around her lit as she looked at them. She had no idea if it was her, the Temple room or her grandma lighting them.

"Here goes," she placed her direct the blank pages of the grimoire. Closed her eyes and thought of her grandmother. The woman she had only met on a few occasions in her entire life. She concentrated extremely hard and imagined lots of foreign words running through her mind. She opened her eyes slightly, peeking to see what if anything was happening. She felt the feel of magic surge through her, and the warmth spread throughout her body. The grimoire seemed to flicker, and a gold light surged from the words on the page, into Cathy and deep into her mind. The lights flickered in the room at the same time, as the grimoire came to life. She concentrated on the photo she had of her grandma, back at her house. She felt it was she, herself saying the words now. Whether she expected sparks, flashes, and fireworks, she gone none of these. Slowly the light and warmth faded away and Cathy felt shattered and almost fainted. Then a strong set of hands held onto held onto her to steady her.

"Hello, my dearest Granddaughter," Cathy turned around to see her Grandma Sally stood in front of her "How can you touch me, are you alive?"

"No, my child, I am a ghost. But the connection between us means you can see, hear me, and touch me. Most people will not be able to see or hear me, although some of the Coven members will be able to though and Harold, of course. Because of you and your new powers, we will be together from now on. Not all the time, but I am only a thought away from you if you ever need me. You are a lot stronger than I could ever have imagined."

"The Coven will be our next step, but before then we will need to practice. But for today, you must rest, you have used a massive amount of energy to bring me back. Let us lock this room and get you a strong coffee, sadly, being a ghost, I can only watch you both." Oskar snuggled as close as possible to Sally. He has his old mistress and his new mistress together at last. "Thank you," he whispered to Cathy.

The strange trio returned to the large lounge that Sally had once shared with Oskar. "I shall stay in this apartment for now," Sally announced, "I will need to get my energy levels back up and I don't feel like running into the Coven members just yet, but I would appreciate if you could text Harold and say Mission Accomplished."

So, for the next hour or two, Sally, Cathy and Oskar sat chatting and catching up on their respective lives.

Chapter 5

The Lessons

After a couple of hectic days running her business and meeting up with Uncle John. She had explained all that had been happening, which he took extremely well. Maybe he knew more than he had ever let on to her?

Cathy was back at the apartment at the mill. She had told the people from her normal world, that she had got her grandmother's unit in the will, and it was mostly empty, so she was going to use it for her online crystal business. She explained her updated website, as part of expanding her business, not that it was done by magic.

She had not yet stayed overnight in the apartment, but Oskar had moved himself back in to be with Sally. When Cathy had sent the mission accomplished text to Harold, he was never away from the apartment, he and Sally seemed incredibly happy to be reunited at last!!

"Hi everyone, I am here for my next lesson," Cathy announced, she always used the shop entrance, so as not to attract any inquisitive questions from the people in the mill. Each day she had been learning, and feeling her body reawaken to her natural witching ways. Since they had been hidden or bound for so long.

"Hallo, Cathy, how good to see you again, we were just talking about you" Harold laughed.

"All good I hope?" Cathy replied, and then saw the look on their faces, and wondered what was going to happen now.

"We both feel that it is time for you to be introduced to the Coven members. Harold got a request from one of them yesterday, and we both feel this could be the appropriate test for you to show the Coven your powers. Yes, it has been a while since I left them, and there is a bit of a power fight going on between a couple of the older members. They need to know that you will be replacing me in the none too distant future."

"Sounds ominous, I don't know how they will take to me replacing you, when and where is this meeting to take place?"

Harold stood up and Cathy could tell by his body language that he was nervous. "The Coven meets in the mill, but not at this apartment, only a few of us know of this, and my apartment in the mill. Yes, I am a little nervous too, as we said since Sally passed, there is always someone wanting to be in charge. Not everyone will be ready to accept you, as a replacement for Sally. They do not know yet that she is, well, back in her current form. So, the evening will be a little awkward in places. It will be fine, as your grandmother left everything set in place for you to be trained by the best of the Coven. We meet in the boardroom of the mill, the one next to the reception. You can imagine there are a few extra flourishes that will appear, what would you expect from a room full of witches and wizards. Today is Thursday, the meeting is to be held on Saturday, at midnight, commonly called the witching hour," as he smiled to himself.

"Cathy," her grandma smiled, "do not look so worried, it will all work out fine, but we will have a few extra lessons today; and up until Saturday. Just so you can understand some of the terminology that is used. I will also explain who is in the Coven, their backgrounds and who is likely to turn up; although I would expect them all to be there to see their new leader. Coffee Cathy? And then to work."

"The Coven is a group of witches and wizards that gather to help the neighbourhood with both paranormal and normal people. They are not a thing to fear, and our Coven is the called the 'Circle of the Dove Stone.' We are a mixed group of people, and the paranormal life around here is quite small – and well behaved. More on that another time, back to the Coven members. We are a group of people that share the same interests, there are other witches in the community that are not part of our Coven, and all the surrounding towns or communities have their own Covens. As I said, we do not have a lot of paranormal activity in our area, but always best to be prepared. Remind me to introduce you to our security guards – Alderman and Alphin, shapeshifters – security by day, giants by night!! people do not mess with those brothers." Sally was in her element discussing the Coven members, the only men being Harold and the Solicitor Roger, the rest a mixture of ages of women,

As Saturday approached, Cathy was learning so much more, spells, about the people in the Coven, traditions, local folklore and of the paranormal creature/people that lived locally.

In the last few weeks of her short life, Cathy's life had literally turned around. She was so thankful that she was divorced from Martin, and not have to listened to his ridicule of what she knew he would say about her magical life. She could go home to her own place whenever she wanted, eat what she wanted and basically do just what she wanted. No mental abuse to worry about, that was all someone else's problem now. She could go out to a meeting at midnight, without having to worry about trying to explain herself to him.

"What do I wear to my first Coven meeting?" Cathy thought aloud, "Casual" her grandmother had now managed to leave the mill and surprised Cathy by being her cottage. "Just be yourself and do not worry, I am with you."

She got back to the mill at 930pm, and had her final lessons in preparation, from Sally. Harold knocked on the apartment door at 11.30pm. He had an apartment on the other side of the emergency hallway, that too, had a door you would walk past if you did not know it was there.

"Are you all set Cathy?" he asked, "are you ready to walk the mill at night? Sorry just joking the lights will come on as we walk by, they are on sensors."

"Will we disturb those living on the top floor?" she asked him. "No, most of them are members of the Coven, so will be at the meeting with us. There are only a few of that do not have an apartment at the Riverside," he explained.

Walking through the maze of corridors got Cathy's anxiety levels rising. She knew her grandmother was with them, but she wanted to reveal herself in her own spectacular style at the meeting. Down one corridor, then another, passing rows and rows of shuttered doors, Cathy wondered what was behind them all. One day she would ask Harold to introduce her to the workers in the units and ask what was in the forbidden cellar!

Eventually they got to the main reception area, where she had arrived just a few weeks ago. The board room was still as impressive, but as you would expect with a room full of witches, it appeared twice the size. The huge table in the centre of the room was full of people sat around it, ordinary looking men, and women, with Roger at the head of the table. There was space for 13 people, Cathy thought that most be the size of the Coven members.

Two of the young women, that she had seen in reception, on her first visit were sat there, they were introduced as Kim and Wendy, sisters, both in their late twenties, like Cathy. The other women sat round the table, ranged from mid-thirties to a couple of women, that looked in their eighties. Cathy was introduced to everyone but knew she would not remember all their names. Roger, who was sat next to her, passed her a piece of paper and it had all the names and were they were sat at the table. "Crib sheet," he smiled at her. "Welcome Cathy to your first 'Circle of the Dove Stone,' Coven meeting."

Chapter 6

The Coven

The room went quiet. Harold stood to address the committee members.

"Ladies and gentlemen, I thank you all for attending this special meeting, with Catherine. As you know she is the granddaughter of our good friend Sally Buckley. It is a pleasure to see you here tonight, Catherine, and I am sure I speak on behalf of everyone here."

Someone coughed and muttered something that Cathy did not quite hear. "Cynthia, have you something to say to us all?" Harold pointedly asked the old woman sat at the far end of the table,

"Well, "she started, "what is an inexperienced girl like her, with no magic, got to do with this Coven. Let alone fill the position that her grandmother left. It should be one of us that takes the place of the leader. She looks like she is scared like a rabbit in headlights, now if Sally were here herself, she would agree with me!" You could tell she had a lot more to say, she looked every inch the image of a wicked witch, and not a nice one at that, maybe she was kind-hearted, but she had just called Cathy a frightened rabbit. She looked a small vicious woman with a huge chip on her shoulder.

"Now then, Cynthia," Roger said very smoothly, "we all know the rules of the Coven, and we must abide by them. Sally left in place her wishes for Catherine to follow her, and we have already seen that she is a very adaptive learner, and that her magic is now unbound and returning quicker than anyone ever thought."

"Umph that remains to be seen, who is teaching her the rules and traditions that our Coven has, you two men? That is more than useless," the old woman was not happy. Roger looked at Cathy and the look told her to remain quiet, as her grandmother was about to make her entrance.

Cynthia and another old woman called Pat, were still talking very loudly, but to each other. The rest of the Coven sat listening to them calling Cathy. They also mentioned Sally's name rather a lot too. Cathy sat listening, quite unsure about what she was getting herself into. The young girls, Kim, and Wendy, who were sat near her, had a very worried look on their faces; as they listened to Cynthia talking about the Coven and how run down it was without a leader and on and on. Just as Cathy felt she had to say something, she felt the chill around her and smiled.

"Ladies," she stood up and put on her most confidence voice she could muster. "Ladies, please could you stop this talk about my grandmother. I know that you want to oversee this Coven yourself, but from what I have learnt, that is not how things work around here." Before she could continue Cynthia was on her feet shouting nonsense and practically spitting with rage. "And who has told you all this, who has been teaching you all of this then?"

"I have Cynthia!" Sally appeared in full sight in the boardroom, most of the witches sat with their mouths open as they saw the very real presence of the former Coven leader. "It is so nice to see some things never change, still as bitter as ever. You did not even give my granddaughter a chance to defend herself, you should be ashamed of yourself. I have been in the room all the time but kept hidden till I thought the time was right, which I am sure it is now. Catherine has been under my guidance from the very first time she stepped into the mill, along with Roger and Harold, we have been collaborating with her."

"How are you here Sally?" Cynthia could only whisper in awe of the life like spectre stood right next to her.

"How do you think Cynthia – that young rabbit over there" pointing to Cathy. "She is the one with the magic, she brought me back, she is the ideal replacement for me. With all your help, she has twice the magic as I ever had, it just needs nurturing."

Desdemona started to cry, she had been close friends with Sally for years and had missed her so much, even witches could get emotional. "I will do my upmost to help her Sally."

"So will I," from the others sat around the table, except Cynthia and just a muffled reply from Pat.

"Ladies thank you. Cynthia and Pat, do we have your backing too?" Sally looked so imposing as she now stood by Cathy.

26

"I have a quest for her, to prove herself," Cynthia shouted, she was not one to give in easily. This must be what my grandma and Harold had been talking about thought Cathy, they had known there was a problem somewhere in the mill.

"What is the quest you have Cynthia," Sally asked, knowing full well what it would be.

"Well. If that girl can bring your ghost visible again, she will be able to get rid of that wretched girl on the top floor. That ghost has been a nuisance ever since I moved her, wailing all night long."

Cathy, quite surprised by this request, just had to ask them. "Why haven't any of you got rid of this girl then?" Sally smiled as she responded to Cathy, "None of them, or I, have your ability to reassure and help the deceased. You showed your power when you made me visible again. This will be the ideal test to start you out on your journey with the Coven,"

Cathy was not quite as sure, but at least it was not having to perform magic tricks for them all,

Roger brought the meeting back to some sort of semblance and the evening continued quite reasonably, everyone was eager to listen and discuss the paranormal activities of the area. The evening even ended with a glass of wine and a small buffet that Kim and Wendy had conjured up.

Cathy chatted to most of the people throughout the evening, keeping her distance from Cynthia and Pat. There were so many names to remember, but she liked the idea of Wendy and Kim being there and future friends.

Eventually people took their leave and Cathy, Sally and Harold made their way back to their apartments. What a strange and good evening that was, Cathy kicked her shoes off as they got into the lounge. "I will stay here tonight, as it is more or less 4 am already".

"Grandma, what can you tell me of this ghost on the top floor of the mill?"

"Tomorrow Cathy, get some rest. I have some business I need to finish off before the night is out, so I will leave you in the capable hands of Oskar. Good night my dear granddaughter."

27

And with that she disappeared. Cathy went to the main bedroom, that had been classed as hers, and climbed into the huge bed. Alongside the ginger cat, that was already snoring loud.

Chapter 7

The Quest is Set

After what seemed like a noticeably short sleep, Cathy stretched out and at first wondered where she was. Then she remembered the meeting and the ghost of the mill. How or what was she supposed to do with a ghost?

She stumbled into the kitchen and thought about her coffee and breakfast, which instantly arrived on the table in front of her, *"How have been missing out from all this magic, all my life she wondered."* As she tucked into her mushroom omelette and rich strong vanilla latte. This could come in handy, she thought, but not to go too foolish, she still needed to keep her figure in check.

As she sat and ate, she thought back to the quest she had been set, what was she going to do, her grandma had not thought it a problem, so hopefully she would help her out.

Just as she was thinking about things, her grandma drifted into the kitchen. "Good, you are up and about, when you have sorted your orders, I want to get started on your quest, I know Cynthia won't rest until it is all sorted and quiet on the top floor."

"What am I supposed to do with a ghost? Cathy asked her grandma.

"That is easy, you must reunite her with her parents, so they can all pass over to the other side together. When people die, they do not always go over right away. They wait to be reunited with their loved ones. We need to speak to the girl and find out what we can and then find her parents and reunite – easy."

"Easy, how easy is that, when did she die, how?"

"That we will find out when we go and talk to her, first you must do your orders and be human" her grandma laughed to herself. "I will be back later, and we will go explore the mill and I will bring Harold, he knows most about this mill."

For the next few hours Cathy busied herself with her crystals and orders. She had moved the stock from her own cottage and now worked fully from the mill unit. Since splitting with her husband and moving into the small house, Cathy had not mixed with her old friends, she always felt they had sided with Martin, so she was very much her own woman.

She had enjoyed the company of Kim and Wendy at the meeting. She looked forward to finding some new friends of her own, with their own quirkiness like hers. The orders were flowing in very nicely. So, Cathy packed every crystal or oils with much love and care as she could. Her favourite crystals were amethysts. Amethyst is said to offer protection, humility, spiritual wisdom, and stress relief. She always carried one or two pieces of amethyst in her pockets, she added another today, she felt she might need the protection.

After a few hours packing and posting, she stopped for a late lunch. Thinking of what her quest was, how do I get out of this one, or should I look at it as a genealogical exercise? Find the family and reunite, even if they have been dead for years, how hard would that be?

At that moment, as if reading her mind, Sally and Harold arrived at the apartment. "Are you ready to go explore Cathy?"

"Don't ghosts only come out at night?" Cathy asked innocently. Her grandmother started laughing so hard she almost cried, "I am a ghost, and I don't just come out at night my dear child."

"Oh, sorry, I don't think of you as a ghost at all," Cathy grinned. "Let's go, but where are we heading?"

"Over by the old lift shaft, then to the top floor, Cynthia lives in one of the small apartments up there, and she says that the girl is always near her apartment," Harold said, leading the way back into the mill. With it being daytime, one or two of the roller shutters were open and Cathy could see inside the small units, one day. When she was not on a mission, she would love to find out more about these people.

Arriving by the lift shaft, Cathy saw that the lift itself must be near a hundred years old, rickety was not in it. "I am not getting into that lift," she said to Harold, he just laughed and pulled the old metal rails of the door back. "Quickest way to the top," and he pressed the button on the lift wall. The experience of the lift was just as Cathy thought it would be, she left her stomach on the ground floor. It would be a while before she did that trip again.

"How do we find the ghost," Cathy asked realising she was going on a ghost hunt, with a ghost.

"That, we are not sure of. No one has ever seen her, just heard the crying and weeping from her, for decades. Therefore, Cynthia thought it would be good for you. But she does not know that you have the genes of a ghost hunter in your blood. Your great grandfather, Sally's father Samuel, was a ghost hunter, but it never passed onto Sally. But we have already seen you have the genes; with the way you got Sally back to us." Harold smiled as though Cathy was their secret weapon.

On arriving on the top floor of the mill, everything seemed very still and quiet. Although that was soon broken, as Cynthia appeared out of her apartment to check who dared enter her top floor of the mill. "Oh, it's just you," she seemed to direct her conversation direct to Cathy.

"Yes, we are here to see if we can find the ghost, that you want rid of," Harold said to her, not in the most pleasant tone of voice. This woman came over to her, as a thorn in his side.

"What can you tell me about this girl?" Cathy asked Cynthia. "I know nothing, except that constant wailing is a nuisance. Show me how good you are then," she challenged. Cathy had no idea why someone could be so nasty, but hey, always an odd one in each bunch,

"Right, we will see you later Cynthia, we have work to do" Harold said to her, walking down the corridor away from her. He headed halfway down the corridor and there was a part of the wall that looked like it had been filled in. "What is this, "Cathy looked at it with interest, she felt a similar breeze around her, like she had when she first felt her grandmothers' ghost.

"This is the old lift shaft, long ago blocked off. Story goes that the girl fell down the shaft and this is where she haunts the mills. No one knows for sure, as the records do not go back that far."

"When are we talking about, approximately. The mill was built around 1850, so when did she die." Cathy's genealogical mind was working overtime now, she loved a challenge, even one like this. "Do you have any clues?" she asked the pair. They have no reply, and so they continued along the corridor.

"I felt a breeze around me when we arrived here," Cathy told them. "Maybe if I hang around a bit, maybe I can get her to talk to me, let her know I am there to help her."

Harold and Sally looked at each other. "Are you sure?" Sally asked, and Cathy nodded. Where she got her bravery from, she had no idea, but felt that she should just be by herself.

"Desdemona lives just down the corridor, we could visit her while you have a scout about," Harold told them. So, it was decided that Cathy go with them, so she knew where they were if she needed them. Desdemona was so thrilled to have them, that they soon forgot about Cathy. So, she left the three of them catching up.

She walked back down the quiet corridor, wondering to herself, where she got her confidence from. She listened carefully for any noises, but she heard nothing; and thought it was probably too early to find the ghost of someone that has been hiding away for years. She stood by the old lift shaft, and again felt a cool breeze around her.

Taking a deep breath, she whispered to herself more than anyone else, "who are you, what is your name, do not be afraid, I am here to help you." The breeze drifted back and forward; Cathy was sure she was not alone anymore. "Can you tell me your name; I want to help you reunite with your parents. But I must hear you first, to start the process off. I know you have been here for many years, but I just want to help you."

Cathy stood very still and tried to tune her mind into the ghost that she felt present with her.

"I know I am new to this, but I can feel you, what is your name? I am only here to help you. Please tell me your name, I know you cry at night, as others have heard you, so you must be able to communicate." Cathy held her breath and concentrated hard. She could feel something but could not tell what it was. "Are you telling me? I can feel you – I can hear something like Clare or something beginning with C – is that your name?"

The breeze swirled round and round her, Cathy knew she had contacted the ghost, now to work out the next steps. After several more tries, Cathy felt exhausted and knew she should conserve her energy, "I will return each day to meet with you, I am sure we can work this out" she talked to the thin air floating around her, "Tomorrow we will try again, please do not be upset, I will do my best to reunite with your parents."

Cathy went back to Desdemona's apartment and the three of the were waiting excitedly for her. "Well, did you feel anything?" Sally asked straight away. "Well, I felt the same cold breeze as I did when I first felt you. So, I talked to what I thought was the girl. I concentrated and tried to get into her head; like you did to me, I am sure she said her name was Clare or began with a C. What does the history or gossip of the ghost call her?"

The three elder witches stared at her. "You said the name began with C or Clare? How did you know that she is known by the mill residents as Clara Jane. You really are a ghost whisperer" Harold looked at her with admiration. "We did not tell you her name, we thought we would help when you needed it or asked for help. The story is that she is around 13 or 14 and worked on the looms and fell down the old shaft, when it was being constructed. No one found her remains, as it was back in the days when the mill was being extended, back in the 1880s. This lift shaft was never completed. With industrial improvements of the time, the bigger lift that is in the mill now, was constructed as it would be able to move the heavy rolls of yarn. So, Clara fell down the unused new construction and eventually the space got filled in and bricked up. Back in the 1960s the ground floor became a store cupboard. The family story that was handed down over the years, was that Clara Jane ran away with her friend, and that is why her parents never passed over until they could find her."

"Well thanks for the help," Cathy felt a bit surprised that they had held this information back from her. "Why couldn't you tell me?"

"Because we wanted to know if you had your great grandfather's genes – as the ghost whisperer and you have beyond doubt proved that is so. What have you decided to do next?" Sally told her.

"I told her I would be back tomorrow. But if her body was never found, she would not have a death certificate. What records do you have for her parents?"

Cathy kind of understood their reasoning, she had already learnt that these people would never do anything bad

33

deliberately, they were just showing her what power she has in herself.

Harold, immediately stepped up with the answers she wanted. "Her parents, we think, were John and Betty Holroyd, they both worked in the mill. Clara Jane was the second eldest of five children. At one stage they all lived in the first cottage across from the loading bay. But after Clara Jane disappeared, the records become non-existent. I know you like the genealogy side of things, so maybe you can fill in the blanks."

The three of them were looking at Cathy as though she held all the answers, Cathy was not quite so sure. "Let me go try again, before we call it a day, with this new information, I want to talk to her and see if she can confirm if it's true about her parents."

She let herself back outside the apartment and went to the lift shaft. "Clara Jane, is that you, are you there, let me know if you can hear me." Cathy was almost knocked over with the rush of breeze that flowed round her, she smiled to herself as she imagined this young girl running round and round her.

"Good, and your parents were John and Betty Holroyd?" Again, the breeze rushed around her.

"Right, I am going researching, I will see you tomorrow, Clara Jane, don't forget I am your friend,"

As her new ghostly friend rushed around her, Cathy caught Harold and Sally's faces watching her from down the corridor. The grins said it all, "Well," she smiled, "looks like the old gossip was correct. But I need to back to my apartment, I am exhausted."

Once back in the apartment, Cathy wrote down all the notes she could remember.

Clara Jane Holroyd aged about 14/15 in the 1880s.

Parents John and Betty Holroyd, lived in the Riverside Mill cottages.

Sally and Harold looked at Cathy scribbling the family tree on her notebook, "I knew you had the magic in you, to do this quest of Cynthia's," her grandmother praised her.

"I have only just started; I have no idea how to reunite them. But for now, I must free that young girl from the horrors of that lift shaft. The elders were so excited that Cathy had managed to make a first contact with the ghost of Clara Jane, they bombarded her with questions about what she felt, and heard.

34

"Let's try the grimoire," Cathy suggested, "let me see if it can help me clear my thoughts about how I go about this quest, as Cynthia called it."

Harold was so excited he kept asking question after question, so Cathy got up to get the grimoire from the Temple room. She heard Harold asking Sally, if she could get one ghost back, surely, she could get another. Sally gently reminded him that she and Cathy had a gene in common and family history, it may not be possible. Harold sat back, he had heard so many complaints in his years in the mill about this ghost and the nuisance some people shouted about. He just wanted to help some poor soul get to the other side.

Cathy finished off her notes before she went to the Temple room. She could not wait to get started on the genealogical side of this adventure. Checking and searching the ancestry websites for census returns and birth marriage etc certificates. She had a sad moment when she recalled there would be no death certificate, as Clara Janes body was never found. She would ask Harold one day about the location, but today was not the time,

Cathy fetched the grimoire from the Temple room, now she just had to touch the door handle and it opened for her. She felt her magic coursing through her every time she stepped into this room. She picked up the grimoire from off the altar. The familiar warm feeling flowed through her as she picked up the book. Many pages were now full of writing, from her many lessons. But still many more lessons and pages to fill in the coming weeks and years.

She took the grimoire back thought to the lounge and asked Sally, what she should do to ask the book to help her. "Go with your heart, ask what it is your mind wants to learn. I am not being awkward, but it is now your grimoire, it will not respond to me now."

Cathy held the book close to her and closed her eyes, while she concentrated, Feeling the spread of magic flowing through her, she relaxed and let the magic do its thing. She concentrated on the quiet voice she heard in her mind, the voice telling her what she must do to help Clara Jane.

"She must get the child to trust in her. This child has been wandering lost in the mill for near 140 years, she has seen people

35

come and go in her mill, no one talking to her, or even listening to her properly. There are probably other ghosts in the old mill, who will also want you to help them pass over, when they know there is a ghost whisper in the building, so Cathy you must concentrate just on Clara Jane. Once she has gained your trust, which may take a while, you need to get her to start talking to you. Eventually you need her to visit the Temple room, so that Sally can help her – one ghost with another.

Whilst gaining her trust, Cathy you must learn all you can about her family history, parents, and siblings. Time to use that certificate you got in genealogy to effective use. Find her parents when they died, where they are buried, so that you can try contact them, and eventually reunite them all.

Once you have Clara Jane's trust, you must learn all she remembers about her family. As she becomes confident and learns to trust you, and understands you are helping. As she visits the Temple room with you her visibility should slowly return. Remember she has been hidden for so long now. Be sure to treat her like an 1880s young mill girl, as she will not have modern understanding, like you have Cathy. In time, the family can be traced to their resting places or place of death, and you must find them, if they have not already passed over. This will work, but it will take time."

When Cathy had relayed all, she heard to Sally and Harold, she was absolutely shattered. Oskar, stirred from his alleged sleeping position, cleared his throat, "Cathy needs to rest. We all know how exciting this is, but we must keep Cathy from running out of her powers by trying too much too soon."

With that direct command from the cat, Sally and Harold retracted, very swiftly, probably across the way to Harold's apartment. Cathy thanked Oskar and curled up on the luxurious sofa, a blanket magically laid over her and she soon dozed off. Dreaming of all the day's events, and the previous weeks, she even pictured what she thought Clara Jane would look like, what would a young mill girl look like from the 1880s.

Chapter 8

The Genealogy

Cathy stretched out and realised she was in her bed at the mill apartment. She remembered falling asleep on the sofa, but not going into the bedroom and undressing. But here she was in her cosy pyjamas, with a very loud snoring cat for company. She checked her watch, and it was 9.45 in the morning. How long had she slept for – and she had eaten nothing!

She got out of her warm bed and grabbed her hoodie off the floor. Walking into the kitchen she thought what she wanted to eat and drink, and when she stepped into the kitchen it was on the table waiting for her. A large mushroom omelette and a large latte, a girl could get used to this. Her notes from last night were on the table next to her, so she powered up her laptop and logged onto the internet.

First things first, check her emails and orders. She told herself she had to put her business first, as that had to keep her going. The ghost whispering and witch ways could not take priority, for now.

Nothing that needed her attention or that could not wait, so she switched onto her genealogy websites and started a new family tree – The Holroyd Family Tree: what did she know?

"John Holroyd married Betty Holroyd.
They had Clara Jane in about 1870.
They lived at Riverside Cottages for a while."

She saved the new tree to her family history site and pressed the search engine to see if anything was there waiting for her. The search engine whirled, then up came the 1881 census for:

1 Riverside Cottage, Green Valley.
John Holroyd Head 40 mill worker b. Green Valley
Betty Holroyd wife 38 domestic duties b. Green Valley

John Junior H son 14 mill worker b. Green Valley
Clara Jane H daughter 12 mill worker b. Green Valley
David Dyson H son ten scholar b. Green Valley
Elizabeth Ann H daughter eight scholar b. Green Valley
Samuel H son Aged three infant b. Green Valley

Cathy could not believe the information she saw in front of her. Amazing that the whole family was there, and at Riverside Cottages. It showed the names of parents, siblings and Clara Jane aged twelve.

From this census Cathy looked for the 1871 census. After a few false starts she soon found them living at The Lakes. This she thought, was a row of cottages about half a mile from the mill. This information told the same, without the children born in the 1870s. Cathy thought that the parents most have married around the time of the birth of their first son, with Betty being called Holroyd in 1871, not a maiden name. Next search, marriages of John Holroyd and a Betty around 1865, in Green Valley.

A few more false starts, and there it was, John Holroyd and Betty Dyson. At Green Valley Parish Church, December 24, 1866. Cathy paid the money and hurriedly printed off the marriage certificate; what an incredible document. Addresses, Ages, Fathers, occupations of everyone. The two fathers of the bride and groom would have been Clara Janes grandfathers, all mill workers, so likely the family was quite poor and the working class of the 1860s society.

Having found her parents' marriage certificate, Cathy decided it was time to find Clara Jane's birth certificate. She knew it was around 1869, so that should not be a challenging task. There were only two Clara Jane Holroyd's in the search for 1869, in the area and ten-mile radius. The only way to find the correct one was to purchase both and print them out.

As the printer hummed whilst printing out the two certificates, Cathy got the first one and shouted to herself, bingo, this was Clara Jane Holroyd, born May 1867 at The Lakes Terrace, but as she printed the second one, it was a replica of the first, same parents, same address but November 1868.

A quick, but sad search of the death certificates, found an infant death for the first Clara Jane, aged only 5 days old. How sad for the parents, their first daughter died and then the second daughter disappeared without a trace when she was 14/15.

Cathy put all the certificates in a folder to keep them dry and safe, and thought just one last search for the 1891 census. She found the various siblings dotted around the village, with their own families or the younger ones with their older siblings. No records of John or Betty on any census return or electoral voters returns.

Searching through the deaths, Cathy found Betty had passed away in 1885 and John in 1886. Paying for the two extra certificates she printed them out and saw that both the same address at time of death was at the workhouse of Green Valley. The workhouse had been at the top of the hill. A lonely, deserted place that was now luxurious apartments. She wondered if any information could be found out about the desolate place. Growing up she had always wondered the type of people that went into the workhouse. Cathy typed all the added information into the tree she felt she had just started; how could she have found so much so quick – magic again.

A coffee fix was needed and a list of what to talk to Clara Jane was what Cathy needed right now. She went on to look at different websites, like the newspapers of the times, and local history websites. Cathy wanted to build as much of a profile of the Holroyd family as she could.

The newspapers did not bring up anything, the disappearance of a mill girl in 1880s would not be newsworthy. The local historical society did have minutes of the workhouse governors, and a mention was noted of inmates that had passed away whilst in the workhouse. Cathy thought it so sad that the poor people were names as inmates. Cathy looked at all her information and wrote out what she had found out so far:

John Holroyd   married 1865   Betty Dyson
Children:
John b 1866
Clara Jane b 1868 died 1868.
Clara Jane b 1868 di 1883/4 approx.
David Dyson b 1871

Elizabeth b 1873
Samuel b 1878

Cathy sorted all her notes into the folder and got back to her online-crystal business. The last few days have been a whirlwind, she felt like she needed so normality. Going into the shop part of her apartment, Cathy had a look at all the stock that needed to be sorted. The delivery had arrived a few days ago and she had totally forgotten about it.

She busied herself with the stock and processed the few orders that were waiting for her. Perhaps she could get an assistant, but who would she trust to work with her in this enchanting shop, at this weird and wonderful mill.

That was a thought for another day, as her mind wandered to what she should ask Clara Jane and how should she handle the trust side of things. Cathy felt she needed to a bit more research about life in the mill in the 1880s, and life in the village or separate hamlets that it was over one hundred years ago. A history lesson as well as genealogical lesson. She thought to herself that Harold would be a good start about the history of the mill and home life in the cottages. She would ask him when she saw him next.

Chapter 9

The Ghosts

Cathy was busy working in the shop. The stock had been cleared away and Cathy was finishing of the last of the orders. When she felt the cool breeze of her grandma around her. She had asked her grandma to make an entrance like this, rather than scaring the living daylights out of her, by just appearing in front of her.

"Good morning, or should I say afternoon, my dearest Catherine. It looks like you have been busy, the shop is a wonderful place now." Sally seemed pleased with herself from the place she had set up, to how Cathy had taken over so naturally, as if it was always there.

"Hi Gran, how are you. I have been so busy this morning", excitedly Cathy told her grandma, "I have found so much about the Holroyd family." And she proceeded to tell her about the infant death, the parents in the workhouse and the siblings.

"You have been busy, although I knew you would be investigating. How ideal that a ghost whisperer should have such an interest in genealogy. I have been thinking also. I know Harold will not be around every time you want to go to the top floor to contact Clara Jane. So, Desdemona and I have been thinking together, and we thought it was time you leant the craft of witch flight!"

"What on earth is witch flight?" asked Cathy. What were they getting her into now?

"Witch flight my dear, will be one of the best things you have ever learnt, but it is a serious secret, so you must be careful where you use it. Witch flight allows you to – well fly from A to B."

"You mean on a broom?" Cathy was inquisitive and a little mischievous.

"Catherine, yes witches do have brooms, and can use them. But witch flight is so much easier. Desdemona and I have thought it would be easier for you to go from the Temple room direct to her apartment. That way no one will see you suddenly arrive. Although, you must message her first, so no sudden surprises." Sally was smiling, as if she knew something that Cathy did not know.

"Tell me more grandma, please," Cathy's interest had suddenly become keen. "I thought no one knew about this place."

"Desdemona was and still is my best friend, we do not have any secrets, she was with me watching you grow up. In fact, her granddaughter, Donna Maria was taken away like you when she was an infant, which may be a search for another day. Dessi came down here often as we worked on spells and the scrying mirrors, we watched you both with. I will explain later about scrying. Dessi is waiting for you now. Come along child, we need to be by the altar for your next lesson."

With that Sally led Cathy back into the corridor and the small door to the Temple room. "Don't look so afraid, it is an easy next step for you now Catherine, you are much more accomplished witch that you think."

The grimoire on the altar was open on a new page, and the letters were sparkling a gold colour. "Read and learn the spell, it really is simple. It will be a great help for you to flit back and forth to your own house," Sally encouraged and smiled; as she knew Cathy would like this part of being a witch.

"Hold your hands tight, think of your destination, leva, leva, levitate, repeat three times. Close your eyes and concentrate."

Cathy looked at Sally, "is that it?"

"Yes, my darling child, that is it. It will use some energy, but stand still, set your intent, concentrate on Dessi and her apartment. And chant the words. I will see you there."

Cathy felt a bit unsure, but did as she was told, her trust in her grandmother was 100%. "Leva-leva, levitate, leva-leva, levitate, leva-leva, levitate, Dessi's apartment," Cathy felt the magic flow through her as she kept her eyes shut closed. Her body began to feel weird, and she felt a whooshing sensation, when she opened her eyes seconds later, she was met with Sally and Dessi grinning ear to ear at her. "I knew it, I knew it," they both danced about. (Which was a bit strange for a ghost and an old witch,)

"Sit down, how do you feel?" they both questioned her. "Dizzy" Cath replied, absolutely gobsmacked that it had worked so easy. "How on earth did that just happen?"

"Magic" they both laughed. "Coffee Cathy, a strong one?" Cathy felt a bit dizzy and sick, what had she just done, how did that happen?

"Wow," was all she could say to Dessi and the ghost of her Grandma Sally.

"Can I do this anywhere?" she was thinking ahead of herself now. Sally replied, "For now, only in the mill – Temple room to Dessi's apartment, but do not forget to warn her. We will work on you going to your own cottage next, but it will take its toll on your magic.

You must imagine you magic is like a battery and using it empties the battery power. For now, drink your coffee and find Clara Jane. Talk to her as if she was in the room with you. Her confidence needs building up,"

Cathy went along the corridor to the old lift shaft; she counted six doors on each side of the corridor and wondered who lived behind the doors. This mill was a whole place of closed doors; and her mind worked overtime to imagine what was behind each door or shutter.

She had only been up to this floor a few times, and this time was a very quick journey up to the top floor, she worked out that it took only a matter of second of time to take the witch flight thru the floors of the old building. As she neared the old lift shaft, Cathy noticed the stillness of the air around her. Was it Clara Jane or was it a sense of nothing was there today?

She checked around her to see if anyone was around, but the corridor was empty. "Clara Jane are you here?" she whispered mainly to herself. Nothing, no rush of air or anything, just the stillness. The air felt odd, what was going on, Cathy asked if Clara Jane was there again, but nothing. Cathy went back to Desdemona's apartment and to see her grandmother's ghost. She did not hang around as she had felt something wasn't right.

"Cathy, you are soon back, what's the problem?" they asked her. She explained what she had felt and the eerie silence. The two good friends looked at each other, it was as though something passed through them to each other, telepathically. "What is it?" Cathy was beginning to worry now.

"We thought this might happen," her grandma said, with a slight tremor in her voice. "The other ghosts in the mill must have realised you are here, and they want you to free them all, but they have no patience. My guess is they have told Clara Jane to be silent until they get their requests seen to. Yes, even in the ghostly world there is bullying still."

"Can we do anything," Cathy began to panic.

"Oh yes, that is why I am waiting in the wings, just in case this happened. OK. Let us go back out to the lift" said Sally, with an incredible look of mischief on her face, and so had Desdemona. They stood, well as much as a ghost could sit. Cathy was a bit taken by surprise, what could they do, that she could not. Well, then again, her grandmother was a ghost herself.

"Let's get ready to battle the ghosts." The older pair laughed. Cathy followed them out of the apartment and down the corridor. At the same time, the door opposite Desdemona's opened and out came one of the other witches from the Coven, the one introduced as Betty Barratt. "Is it happening at last?" she asked excitedly, "Come on" said Dessi.

"What exactly is going on", said Cathy running after the three of them "Sally stopped and waited for Cathy, "We have known there are a few ghosts in the mill. I have been trying to find them since I passed. They are the ones that are the nuisances, not Clara Jane. They have pried on this poor girl for too long. We have prepared a banishment spell for years, but we needed your magic to draw them out. Once we get rid of them, Clara Jane will be able to reveal herself and then we can help her."

"How do I come into this?" Cathy was a little more panicked now. "It is nothing really Cathy, we have it all in hand. We just need you to call upon the two main trouble causes, you just have to ask them to come forward and how can you help them, we will do the rest."

Betty put her hand on her arm, "Trust us, we know what we are doing, we have what we need in the bags." Cathy had not noticed the bags they were carrying. But as they got near to the lift shaft, Cathy felt the air was no longer still, but quite disturbed. Another couple of the witches came out of their apartments, and

Cathy smiled as she realised, they were Edith and Mary from the Coven, although there was no Cynthia or Pat present.

Betty and Desdemona drew some lines on the corridor floor and lit some black candles. Cathy watched as these old witches practised their craft.

"Right Cathy," her grandmother instructed where she should stand and the words, she needed to repeat to the ghosts that they wanted her to bring out.

Cathy said the words, over and over, she did not quite understand, but after a few minutes she felt a horrible rush of cold freezing air wrap around her, her head was full of voices that she had never heard before.

During them, she could hear her grandmother and friends chanting in, what sounded like Latin.

The air around felt like she was suffocating, and she felt she was being lifted into the air. She was scared now, and just kept repeating the words here grandmother told her to say. After what felt like hours, she dropped to the floor. Cold and shaking she felt like she had passed over herself. She lay still on the cold floor with her eyes close. Cathy just felt she could not move; her battery was flat.

Cathy felt someone put a warm blanket over her and slowly opened her eyes. The Coven members were stood around her. Sally came forward and help Cathy to sit up. Desdemona brought her a strong warm coffee, what was in it she did not know but it tasted odd.

She took a sip and asked nervously if they had been successful. "Oh yes" the witches all cackled together. "Four of those bad buggers gone to rest for eternity," one of them said.

Suddenly, Cathy could hear something else. From the corner of her eyes, she could see a slight figure sat by the old lift shaft. Shivers ran down her spine. "Err can anyone see someone near the lift shaft?"

"What do you mean?" Sally asked. Cathy slowly got up and walked to the slight figure sat curled up by the lift shaft.

"Clara Jane is it you?" she asked gently to the weeping figure. "Can you see me?" the child wept. "I can faintly make your shape out."

Sally floated over to the pair. She sat beside Clara Jane and put her arms around the weeping child. "You are safe now; we have banished the four bullies from the mill. You can trust Cathy now; she will help you reunite with your family. "

Cathy looked on in amazement, the more Sally talked to this poor mill girl from the 1880s, the more her shape became clearer. Two ghosts from different centuries holding each other.

Sally explained to Cathy and Clara Jane what had just happened. The Coven knew that there were a few of the older ghosts that were very unhappy with their lot, but none of them wanted to pass over to the afterlife.

George had died in the 1850, aged forty-three due to one of the old looms in the mill collapsing on him. Bob was a few decades later in 1875, he had had a heart attack in the packing area, and he had refused to leave the mill. Tommy and Fred had both died during the first world war. They had been loading a truck with ammunition when the load caught fire. It exploded, killing them both in the loading bay area.

The older ghosts Bob and George had recruited the two young lads from 1917 and they had become kind of like the ghost mafia of Riverside mill. Research had been done before on these four men, and it turned out all of them had been grumpy miserable single men in life and the same in death. The Coven had known they existed and when Sally had passed, she made it her mission to rid the mill of them. But they had been missing one link, a ghost whisperer. Cathy had been a godsend and now the men were safely passed onto the other side. The mill would be a better place now for its resident ghost community and the living tenants too.

Cathy was shocked that her own powers could have done all this. She watched as Clara Jane seemed to soften and curl up next to Sally. A slight pang of jealousy passed over her, as she had never curled up with her grandmother like that, but now was not the time to get selfish. She had her grandmother now, and a whole new family was forming with the rest of the Coven.

Chapter 10

Cynthia

"What's going on here" a voice screeched from the other end of the corridor. Everyone turned to find Cynthia standing outside her apartment waving a rolling pin around, "Calm down Cynthia" Desdemona told her, "Cathy has been working on the quest you set her at the Coven meeting,"

"Huh, well that will never happen, that ghost is just a plain nuisance, always has been ever since I moved in this place." She scoffed.

"Cynthia," Desdemona replied, "You know full well the nuisance has not been the young girl, but the ghost bullies that have roamed the mill for decades."

"So, you say, but what is she going to do about it?" Cynthia cackled back at her.

"Well, on that matter, you have just missed all the fun. We set in place the spell; just has we have discussed on many occasions. Then, the superb Catherine with her magical powers called the four of them – yes, the four bullies that have made this mill a misery for year, she called them to the circle. Like the stupid men they are, they felt straight into the trap. Tommy, Fred, George, and Bob have all passed over peacefully now. It took a lot out of Cathy, but you can find her near the lift shaft, for your apology." Desdemona pointed to Cathy and the ghosts.

"Who is that with them? That young girl? Is it who I think it is!" Cynthia could not contain herself anymore. Tears flowed through her small eyes, and everyone looked so confused.

"What is it, Cynthia?" asked Betty, she had never seen Cynthia like this. "Tell us, why are you so sad, now the bullies have moved on."

Cynthia walked over and came and sat by Cathy and Sally. "Clara Jane, I can see you now, I want to tell you how much your family missed you. They thought you had run off with that bad lad, and could never understand why. I am your great niece, your brother Samuel had a son, and he was my father. I am so sorry I never believed the story that it was your ghost that was in the mill. You ran away, tell me what happened that you are still here in the mill."

Clara Jane looked at everyone and snuggled deeper into the ghost of Sally, she looked scared, if that was possible for a ghost.

"Leave her be for a while, everyone," Cathy told them. "All back to your apartments please. I will look after Clara Jane with Sally, and Cynthia, please could you let me have any family history that you know, so that the family can be reunited."

Cynthia looked quite shell shocked herself and seem to have run out of words. "Come along, Cynthia" Betty said leading Cynthia back to her own apartment. "A strong cup of tea is what you need right now."

Eventually the witches had all returned to their apartments, except Dessi, who was an important member of this small group. "Let's go to my apartment and see what we should do next."

Sally coaxed the shaking, weeping girl to her feet and led them to Desdemona's apartment. Cathy held to the back of the group, wondering what to do next, the girl was so scared, would she ever get back to anything like normal for a ghost, and to have Cynthia as a great niece, unfortunate thing, but it would help greatly with the research. Cathy did not blame Cynthia for not mentioning anything, as she seemed genuine when she found out the child was her relative.

Following the others into Desdemona's comfortable apartment; Cathy sat in one of the comfortable chairs and wanted to curl up herself. But she knew the quest now, had only just begun. Cathy noted that Clara Jane was wearing the grey smock that she had dreamt about the other night, "Clara Jane, have you been visiting my dreams, as I feel like I have seen you before."

Very quietly, Clara Jane uttered her first words to the group, "When you called me the other day, I could see you and feel that you are different than the other people that live in the mill. I felt hope at last. I did not visit you, but I kept thinking of you over and over, so maybe that is what happened."

"Are you ready to tell me what happened Clara Jane?" Cathy asked quietly. All the time Clara has clung to Sally like a life jacket.

48

"I didn't fall down the lift shaft, I was pushed" Clara Jane let that bombshell sink in. "It was not an accident, I was pushed. By Marty, the one that everyone thought I had run away with. Well, he thought it was funny and he pushed me. I lay in the dark lift shaft for days, the pain eventually gave in. No one heard my screams for help. It was so dark, I shut my eyes and willed myself to die, it did not take me long.

Eventually, as a ghost I could float around, but always stayed close to the lift shaft. Even in death I was still scared of the other ghosts. That Bob made me cry so many times, they teased me that no one loved me and that is why I was not found, years and years of misery,"

Clara Jane broke down into floods of tears, still in Sally's arms. "Marty ran away because he knew what he had done, He did not tell my parents what had happened, even though we only lived across the way, he was a coward. I tried to visit my parents, but my mother thought she was going mad and seeing things. She could not hear me, but I think she could see me. I just wanted the truth to be known. But then they moved, and I do not know what happened to them."

Cathy held back about the workhouse, now was not the time. "What do we do now?" she asked. Sally replied that it was time to go back to our apartment and take Clara Jane with us.

"Are you up to a witch flight or would you rather walk?" Sally asked. "Clara can come with me, I will show her the nice parts of the mill now, until the time comes for us to decide what happens next."

"I will walk, my legs are weak from all the power I have used, but I don't want to feel sick again from the witch flight. I will meet you downstairs." With that Cathy thanked Desdemona for her hospitality and in return Dessi gave her a massive hug and thanked her for ridding the mill of the unwanted ghosts. "You are incredibly special Cathy, do not ever forget that. The powers you used today, well, few people can do that. Keep learning my child. You will be all that Sally was, and more."

Cathy left the three of them in the apartment and made her way back to the staircase at the end of the corridor, she felt like she wasn't alone, as the air swirled around her, "Is anyone there?" she whispered.

Suddenly, before her was a couple of faint outlines, of what she thought were women, middle aged but she was not sure.

"We want to thank you for ridding the mill of those men. We have all lived here many years, and they made life or death, awful with their bullying," she laughed at her own joke. "We will not be any trouble, but please look after young Clara Jane, she was murdered, while the rest of us lost our lives through one accident or illness. Like the Spanish Flu finishing us both off. Please remember Cathy, what your grandmother Sally told you, not all ghosts are bad. If you ever need us, just call, we will be your servants for all time now, thank you again, I am Pearl and the quiet one is my sister Ruby. Thank you, Cathy, our enchanted mill will be peaceful now."

With that, Pearl and Ruby disappeared back into the ether and Cathy, still in shock at all that was happening to her, made her way back to the mill apartment.

Chapter 11

Clara Jane

When she got back downstairs, which was an uneventful trip after the ghosts' thank you. Cathy found Sally and Clara Jane in the lounge, already Clara Jane looked slightly happier. Still next to Sally, they hovered just above the sofa. It was odd to see two alive looking people, which were ghosts. Yet they could touch each other, that was amazing. Cathy told the two of them about her visitation when she had left the top floor apartment. They had both heard of Ruby and Pearl, they had both come across them in the mill.

"The older ghosts kept away from the areas of the bullies, but maybe now the mill will settle into a more relaxed place," Sally told them.

"Cathy, why do not you show Clara Jane your shop, I am sure she would love to see your crystal collection, you will have to explain what it all is. We must remember that Clara Jane passed away back in 1883. I have a couple of jobs I need to do. Clara Jane, you will be fine with Cathy, she is my granddaughter and just a younger version of myself." With that Sally disappeared.

"Hi Clara Jane, would you like to see my shop. You will have to tell me what your home life was like, I have done a little research and know two of the houses that you lived in, when you are stronger, we can go and look around outside. Until then, let us make you at home here, with me and Sally.

Cathy led Clara Jane down the small corridor and into her shop of crystals, "Oh my," what are all these stones? With that Cathy set about showing Clara Jane all her favourite ones, and the ice was broken between the two of them. Even with over one hundred years between them, the love for the crystals was always deep inside most people.

Cathy watched as Clara Jane went from one shelf to another, feeling the crystals and asking questions. Cathy laughed to herself, as she thought how much a help someone like Clara Jane could be in her shop, but how would you teach a ghost from 1883 how to use a computer.

After, what seemed like ages, Cathy and Clara Jane went back into the kitchen. Cathy was in desperate need of food. Clara Jane was busy looking at all the modern appliances. Asking what things all along the way were. Cathy explained as best she could how the microwave worked, the kettle, electricity.

Clara Jane was very quick at learning, she even recognised cheese and bread and they laughed that some things had not changed at all. Seeing this young mill worker had lived in a tiny house with her parents and four siblings, back in the 1870/80s, she was intrigued with the technology. She explained to Cathy, that with being in the mill for so long, she had seen things change from her times. It was looking like she had kept up quite well with modern advancements.

"Will I be able to wear clothes like you?" she asked Cathy, who was wearing her jeans, boots, and jumper. "I will have to ask my grandmother, she seems to change outfits, so maybe it will be possible, it would keep you warmer."

"Oh, I do not get cold, it is one advantage of being a ghost," Clara Jane actually laughed.

After just a few hours, Cathy was thinking of Clara Jane as a younger sister. She just seemed so familiar to her, maybe her own ancestors had been friends with her, when they had been alive. So much to learn from this walking history lesson. She hoped they would be able to help her reunite with her parents.

When Clara Jane had been living, she had shared a small cottage with her parents and siblings. There were no bathrooms in these houses, just a privy in the back that was shared by the cottages and a kitchen sink to get washed in. The old tin bath was used sometimes, but lots of water had to be boiled on the bungalow range fire in the cottage, which also did most of the cooking. In her years as a ghost, she had seen the invention of electric lights, further inventions of the industrial revolution and even the technical revolution. She had seen the children disappear from the workplace and heard that they went to school each day. She had been to school a little, but like everyone else in Green Valley at the time, she went to work in the mill when she was nine.

She had seen local people working the looms and then foreign people in the 1970s, and she didn't understand their language. She had been scared in 1967, when the top floor of the mill had set on fire, but Pearl and Ruby had looked after her even then. The mill had survived, because the floors were solid, rather than a wooden floor. Clara Jane had been worried what would happen if the mill had burnt down, but the other two encouraged her that they would still be able to find somewhere else to haunt.

After some food and a rest, while Clara Jane went back to the shop and carried on looking at the crystals, Cathy sat wondering just how much the ghost had become almost alive in such a short time. Like Sally, she could touch some things, her form was now a solid body, like Sally's. What sort of magic do I possess?

When Sally got back to the apartment, she found Cathy asleep and wondered where Clara Jane was. Listening hard, she heard a sweet voice singing from the shop area. She followed the voice and found Clara Jane singing to herself, surrounded by crystals of all sorts. She was sat cross-legged, just hovering over the shop floor.

"Is everything alright Clara Jane?" Sally quietly asked her, so as not to startle her.

"Oh yes," the young girl looked up at Sally, "what do I call you, it is not manners to call you by your Christian name. I have not forgotten my manners in all these years Miss,"

"Oh dear, that's a question to ask, everyone calls me Sally, except Cathy who calls me Grandma," Sally thought hard, she could not be gran or aunt, and she certainly was not being Mrs Buckley again, "Maybe for now, just call me Miss, eventually we will find a name for me and the other Coven members. Did you know that there was a Coven of witches at the mill?"

"Oh yes, Miss, I have followed the activities for years. I think I might have been a witch if I had been allowed to grow up. Cathy said you may help me get a change of clothes too. I have worn this smock for a bit too long now." She would have liked to have one of those new-fangled showers too but knew that was not possible now.

"What would you like to wear, Clara Jane, something like Cathy wears, although girls in trousers is still very modern!" Sally was very sympathetic to this young ghost, which had been hidden away for so many years. "Oh yes please, how do I change, will you teach me how to be a modern ghost please.

Sally smiled and said, "let's go wake Cathy, she is the one with the magic. I can help anything ghost wise; and Cathy is for the magical journey we are all on."

"Cathy darling, we need some help please," Sally gently disturbed Cathy from her slumbers, "What help do you need Gran," sleepily she uncurled her body, "Oh, I do feel better after a sleep."

"Yes, you have recharged your battery now. We need to go to the Temple room; I have an idea that might help Clara Jane adapt her clothing."

Leading the way back down the corridor, Cathy caught sight of the piles of crystals on the floor in the shop, she smiled to herself, and thought about the work of putting them all back. As if reading herself, her gran whispered, "magic will clear it all up later, don't worry."

Clara Jane was struck dumb when they entered the special Temple room. The grimoire on the alter was flashing, as if calling to Cathy. "Look Gran, I am being called already, come on Clara Jane, lets finish your conversion from hiding away, to a modern young lady ghost."

Skipping behind Cathy, Clara Jane could not believe what was happening to her after all this time. This room was amazing, some things she recognised from her mother's own kitchen. "We had a pot like that she said, looking at the pestle and mortar. And one of those and mum had a book of recipes that looked like that one."

Sally took Clara Jane's arm and said to her "You must not come in here alone, the room won't let you, but you must not try. This is Cathy's Temple room now, and she is still learning. You must only be with Cathy when this room is open – never alone."

Cathy and Sally set the grimoire on the altar and looked at the page, it was open at, "looks like this is the spell for Clara Jane to dress herself," Cathy said and began the spell to transform the young ghost.

"Have I been missing out" a voice called from the doorway. Oskar stood there; he looked like he had been chasing rodents all night.

"Where have you been? We have had an adventure this afternoon. We have banished the four bullies of ghosts, from the mill and this young lady is Clara Jane."

Cathy told the cat. Clara Jane was still working out how the cat spoke to them. "He is my familiar, all witches have a familiar, mostly cats, but other animals can be familiars, Oskar was my grandmothers familiar before mine."

Oskar looked at them all, and when he spoke, he said, "I know you did, I was watching from Stephen's apartment." He looked quite smug, if a little filthy in his fur.

"We were watching you and saw what happened. But you know how eccentric old Stephen is. He is the one that carries his stuffed cat around with him. He was a detective in his younger days; a magical detective that worked for the magical police agency or MPA as he likes to call them. He was interested to see that the old folklore of Clara Jane falling down the lift shaft was true, that he had me and him go down to see if we could get into the base of the old shaft, hence why I am so horribly scruffy."

"What did you find?" they all cried at once. "Nothing but an old cleaning cupboard at the base of the shaft, but it did look like the floor had been filled in with something years ago. Stephen thinks we should call in the local police to see if they can shed any light on how we can get to the remains of poor Clara Jane."

"Would that be possible?" Clara Jane was a little taken aback, she never thought that her remains could have a proper burial, maybe with her parents, after all this time.

"Cathy, it would be up to you to ask, or maybe we could see Harold, as he oversees the mill. We are two ghosts and a talking cat," laughed Oskar.

"Let me ring him and get him over here. We will need to call a meeting of the Coven, to see what the other people suggest. We cannot just start to dig up the bones. But how do we tell people we have basically rescued a ghost?" Cathy was hesitant but excited too.

Chapter 12

The Coven

It was agreed to call Harold, and then a Coven meeting was arranged for the following Saturday night, at midnight, as usual.

In the meantime, Cathy and Clara Jane worked in the shop. Cathy was teaching Clara Jane all about the properties of each crystal. They were pretty, but also powerful used in the correct way.

Clara Jane was now dressed in jeans, like Cathy. But she went for the blouse and cardigan look, as her mother always wore a blouse and cardigan for church on a Sunday. Her Sunday best she had called them. The days passed quickly, and Cathy was glad of the company, and the fact that Clara Jane seemed to love the crystals as much as she did herself, and the hundreds of customers she kept supplied.

While they worked, Cathy got Clara Jane up to date on what she had found out about her family tree, and carefully mentioned that her parents had both died in the workhouse. Surprisingly, that news did not seem to bother her as much as she had expected. Then Clara Jane told her that all poor people ended up going to and dying in the workhouse. She also told Cathy that she had been friends with the daughter of the workhouse. They had gone to Sunday School together; she thought her name had been Betsy.

Sometimes Cathy caught Clara Jane staring into space and asked her what she was thinking. It was usually of her parents and siblings.

Cathy could not believe that the old woman called Cynthia, was a grandchild of her younger brother. He had only been a small child when she had her accident. Clara Jane told Cathy that over the years, she had watched her family grow up and leave the mill yard. She had never ventured out of the mill, after her mother and father left. Maybe one day she would get the courage again. Cathy agreed that they would venture outside the mill one day, in preparation for reuniting with her parents.

By the time Saturday arrived, Clara Jane looked just like a young modern teenager. She had been just fourteen when she had died. Sally had also taken her under her wing. While Cathy slept at night, Sally had been teaching Clara Jane the ghostly does and don'ts.

Harold called for Cathy at 11.30pm, like before, He had met Clara Jane after Cathy had phoned him and he had nipped round. (Although he never needed an excuse, when he knew Sally was there).

The four of them, and Oskar this time, made their way through the mill, and to the boardroom. Clara Jane stuck close to Sally, as this was her first time in the office block. It still intimidated her; she had only ever been in once before and that was because she had been told off for being late one day. *"The old mill managers were not like today's managers,"* she thought.

The board room was full, everyone from the Coven had attended, and the formalities were done, introducing Clara Jane to everyone.

Cynthia came over to Cathy and Clara Jane, cleared her voice and announced "Ladies and gentlemen, I have a big announcement to make. I would like it to be witnessed, that I owe Cathy a huge apology and I thank her for all she has done. Bringing the building back to peaceful times. Without her, we would not be here meeting to discuss the future of this young lady. Clara Jane, I have a present for you, I have put together everything I know about our shared ancestors. I will give it to Cathy for her to go through with you, when the meeting is over. Thank you again Catherine, Sally was right, you are going to be as good as she ever was. I think we have only seen the beginning with you so far."

Everyone gave Cynthia a round of applause, it was exceedingly rare she ever admitted that she could have been wrong. A knock came to the boardroom door, and a very eccentric elderly gentleman came into the room, clutching, what appeared to be a small stuffed cat. "Thank you for inviting me down, Harold. To those of you that have not met me, my name is Stephen. I am a former detective with the MPA. I am here to offer any help I can in putting this young lady remains to rest."

Dressed in a three-piece suit, complete with bow-tie, the elderly gent sat next to Harold and Roger.

"Right, that is everyone is here now, welcome to our new guests, Wendy and Kim, could you please get seated, Clara Jane will be here after the meeting for you to chat to." The young girls both blushed and went to take their seats at the large table,

"Tonight, we have called this meeting, to discuss the events of the last week. To try to find the bodily remains of this sweet young girl. In the hope that she can be laid to rest with her parents. Now due to some good detective work by Stephen, Hamish, and Oskar. We know that the base of the lift shaft was covered with rubble when the lift was being built. This is where we believe we will find the remains, but we cannot just go digging. It will have to be done under the guidance of the magical police agency, Stephen has kindly said he would introduce us all to his son and grandson. They are also in the police agency if it is totally agreed by the Coven members?"

Everyone agreed, as it seemed only fitting to help Clara Jane's remains be laid to rest. The whole Coven had taken to the young girl. Her life and death had been so tragic, that whatever anyone could do, would be the best they could. So, it was arranged for Cathy, Roger, and Harold to go meet Stephen's son, Brian, at his offices the very next day.

The members of the Coven were all different from the last time Cathy had met them, they were so much more friendly, even Pat and especially Cynthia. It seemed that the banishing of the four ghosts had eased the atmosphere of the whole building itself, and its occupants.

Wendy and Kim got the buffet started and the kitchen adjacent to the board room was buzzing. Everyone was updating each other on what they had been doing, new spells, spells that had gone wrong. But none seemed to be as impressive as Cathy banishing the four ghosts.

After everyone had eaten their fill and drunk enough, they started to drift away. Stephen and his stuffed cat made his way over to her. "Cathy, I must say you have done a marvellous job already in your young career as a witch. Should you ever need anything, just let me know, I am at your disposal." She felt he was a bit too close for comfort, but as she brushed past the stuffed cat, she felt that it was warm, and not just stuffed. Stephen smiled. "A story for another day my dear, we all need to go and get some sleep, we have a visit with another detective or two, tomorrow."

Cathy remembered the meeting with the magical police and wondered what was going to happen next to her in this weird but wonderful journey she was taking.

As she was taking her leave, Kim and Wendy caught up with her. "Cathy," Kim shouted, and they raced over to her. "We are going to the music festival in the field, next weekend, would you like to come with us? It is only at the local sports field, and a few tribute acts, but we thought it would be good for you to have a "normal "day, with us both."

Cathy felt like she had not been out socialising for ages, since before her divorce. "That would be great, thank you for asking me. I will look forward to that very much" she replied.

"Call in reception through the week and we can decide how we will get there, no magic allowed," the two young women left together, nattering away to each other. Cathy smiled as she watched them go, she had always missed having a younger or even an older sibling.

Rounding up Sally, Harold, and Clara Jane, (who was sat with Cynthia, like they had known each other for ever,) they made their way back through the maze of corridors back to her apartment. She was glad that Harold escorted her, as she was sure she would still get lost, even though she had been in the mill for over a month now.

Chapter 12a
(Chapter 13 is unlucky for some)

The Detectives

Cathy woke late in the morning, after the midnight meeting, she was not going to rush. It had taken her a while to get to sleep, she seemed to stay at the mill more than her own cottage these days. She lay in her king size bed and thought how so much had happened to her in such a brief time. She was now living, in an enchanted mill, with two ghosts and a talking cat.

The meeting with the police was scheduled for 3pm, and both Harold and Eccentric Stephen were going with her. They were going to ask how they go about uncovering the remains of Clara Jane, from the old lift shaft. Apparently, you just could not start digging up murdered bodies form 140 years ago. Cathy wondered what Stephen's son Brian was going to be like, a younger version of his dad. Thinking about Stephen, that cat was something else, what was going on there? She would have to find the underlying cause of that too.

As was her usual pattern of work nowadays, Cathy got up, magicked her coffee and breakfast, a quick shower. Sally had shown her the spell of getting dressed in the click of her fingers. New clothes were accessible without even shopping these days. Just imagine what you want to wear, and voila. After her late breakfast, she made her way to the corridor that went to her shop, the shop door was open, which kind of worried her, but she could hear Clara Janes sweet singing voice and Oskar trying to join in!!!

"Good morning you two, how are we all today?" Cathy announced herself as she went into the shop area. So far it was still just an online business, maybe one day she would open to the public, but not yet.

"Oh, good morning, Miss Cathy," Clara Jane now called her, and Miss Sally, it made her feel better. "When you have a chance, can we go through the box that Cynthia gave to you last night, as

I can't hold onto much just yet, with being a ghost, except the crystal, Oskar tries to help but he just knocks the box over."

"Of course," Cathy had left the box on the lounge table when they had eventually returned from the Coven meeting earlier in the morning, "We can put it with my information and then we can start looking for your parents grave or hopefully their ghosts."

"Cathy," Clara Jane began, "I have been thinking, could I look through the box with Cynthia, I know you are busy, trying to sort my things out. Well, Cynthia is my relative, and she is very lonely."

"What a great idea, I will get my research too and we can go and visit Cynthia before I go to the police, with Stephen and Harold," Cathy replied. "Shall we go now?"

Cathy decided it would be easier to walk up to the top floor, and Cynthia's apartment, she did not want to use her witch flight ability too often. With Clara Jane was alongside her, she hesitantly knocked on Cynthia's door.

"Well, what a surprise, you two being here" Cynthia said to them both.

"Hi Cynthia," Cathy smiled nicely, she still did not trust this woman. "Clara Jane wondered if you would go through the box of family history, that you gave me last night. She wants to get to know you better, as you are her only family. I have also brought my research for you to look at. So maybe between us we can find out the resting place for her parents,"

"Oh my," the old woman was overcome, it looked like she did not get many people wanting to be friends with her, even though Clara Jane and Cynthia had chatted at the Coven meeting last night. "Oh, come on inside," Cynthia invited them into her apartment.

Cathy was quite taken aback with the size and neatness of this apartment; each one was different than the others. Cathy told her that she could not stop, as she had to go the appointment with the magical police. In order to get the permission to start the excavation of the lift shaft.

"Can I leave Clara Jane with you, whilst I am out?" she asked Cynthia.

61

"Absolutely, come on in my child, please make yourself at home, as best as you can, let us get started, shall we? We have a lot to catch up on, and I will explain who is in the photographs, I have found for you."

Cathy left them together and made her way back down to her apartment, she was so surprised with Cynthia's reaction, she felt she must make more time to meet all the Coven, away from the meetings, to get to know them better. At least Clara Jane would be with someone and not worrying about the talk of finding her remains, for any ghost that could not be a nice thought.

Back at the apartment, Cathy finished the orders and set about getting ready for the trip to the magical police agency. She wondered what to expect, so many things had happened to her lately. She had no idea, but she assumed it would be a formal meeting to gain approval to excavate the lift area. Hopefully to find the remains of Clara Jane after so long. It was time she was laid to rest, although she had got used to having her ghost around already.

2.30pm her companions rang her to let her know they were waiting outside, so she grabbed her bag and coat and went out the shop door to the waiting car. Harold was driving and Stephen was sat in the back. "Where is Hamish?" she asked quietly, she thought that Stephen took Hamish everywhere. "Oh, he is with your Oskar, he always stays with him when I am going out." He replied.

"Can I ask about Hamish?" Cathy hesitated. "Is Hamish alive, I passed him last night and he felt warm to touch?" She was quite embarrassed to ask this question, but curiosity won her over.

"Do not be embarrassed Cathy, yes Hamish is alive, he is in fact an older brother to your Oskar. But the unfortunate thing is quite old now and nearly blind, hence I carry him all around. It is a game he plays; he likes pretending to be a toy and making people think I am even more eccentric. Few people know about him, as he does not go out of the mill. He is also my familiar, like Oskar is to you, and previously your grandmother, wonderful cats both. Oskar spends a lot of time with Hamish, helping him around the apartment, when I go out."

Cathy did not know what to say, she was speechless, yet again, what a fabulous compliment to Oskar.

"Here we are at the agency," Harold announced as he parked the snazzy sports car. "We shouldn't be too long, a case of formalising the arrangements to proceed with the excavation" Stephen led the way to his son's office, the lady on reception just waved them through to the back of the office.

Coming to a glass door, Stephen just lightly knocked and walked straight into the larger than expected office. Sat behind a desk was a man that looked in his early sixties, and next to him a young man about her own age. "Hi dad" the older man said. Stephen went over and shook hands with them both, "Brian how are you son, and I see you have brought Adam in too, how is my eldest grandson doing?" Harold took his hand too and then did the introductions.

He turned to Cathy, smiling like the proud father he was, Cathy this is my son and grandson, it is a family tradition that we all work for the magical police agency. Boys, you know Harold, and this is Cathy, Sally's granddaughter. She has returned to the Coven, finally. She has been an amazing asset to the mill, and that is why we are here today. Cathy is the one that instigated the removal of the nuisance ghosts at the mill and freeing the young ghost of Clara Jane. Hamish, Oskar, and I have a clever idea where the remains of Clara Jane are. But we know we need the appropriate approval from the police to start the process. Cathy has researched a lot of her family, and it turns out that old Cynthia is a descendant of her brother. The idea is to find her remains and give her a decent burial. Will it be a problem?"

Brian, stood up, "it should not be a problem dad, so long as we follow procedure. We will need to be with you while the excavation takes place. If we do find anything the coroner will be involved. Did you say that she said she was pushed, by a friend?" he asked.

"Yes, that's what we have been told us," Stephen answered.

Adam now joined in the conversation, "Well in this case, it will be an historical magical murder investigation. I will start the paperwork going and inform the authorities. I will get in touch when we can proceed. Nice to meet you Cathy," and with that the meeting was over,

"Shall we adjourn and get a coffee? Adam piped up, "what *a voice*" thought Cathy to herself, and felt her cheeks start to blush.

She had not thought like that for over a year – well longer since her ex was found out to be such an idiot and gold digger. "That sounds a good idea," she replied, a little too quick, and found herself blushing.

"Let's go to the small café down the road" suggested Brian, jumping in to rescue the pair of them. "We can discuss our next move there." The five of them walked down the road to the small coffee shop and ordered a variety of cakes and coffees,

Continuing the conversation from the office, the young detective, said "We will have to make this an historical project Cathy, as the crime took place over one hundred years ago. I will inform the County Archaeologist in the morning. Also, the building is of historical interest, so it is a double whammy, I am afraid. Once I have been in touch with him, I will give you a ring, to sort out meeting up at the mill. If you let me have your phone number." This time it was Adams turn to blush. Cathy handed him one of Crystal Cave business cards, and as their hands brushed against each other, she felt the magic spread through her again. *"What just happened there?"* she thought to herself.

"We best get back to the mill soon, I do not like to leave Hamish too long," Stephen spared their blushes this time round.

"I will get in touch as soon as I have heard back from Peter, the archaeologist." Adam said, whilst staring just at Cathy, and with that they all left the coffee shop and back to their normal business.

Chapter 14

The Site Visit

Cathy could hear her phone ringing, and thought to herself, *"who could be ringing at such an unearthly hour?"* She looked at her phone, it was only 8.30 in the morning. After the meeting yesterday, she had gone back to her cottage to catch up on her sleep, late night Coven meetings and the past few months were taking its toll on her. She could not imagine how much her life was changing. Reaching out, she grabbed her phone and answered the unknown number, "Hi Cathy here."

"Hi Cathy, its Adam, Stephen's grandson. We met yesterday. I know its early, but I messaged Pete the archaeologist last night, and he got back right away. He eager to get on with a proper investigation. He needs to look at the site, so we can assess what paperwork needs to be approved and what measures we need to take to get the excavation going. Could you meet us at the mill, say around midday? And err, would you like to go for some lunch with me afterwards?"

Cathy smiled to herself; he must have felt the same magic. After all his grandfather was a wizard, maybe he was too.

"Sure, that sounds a good idea to me too." Cathy replied to him, already planning the outfit she would be wearing. "Midday gives me plenty of time to process the orders and sort the queries; and be at the mill on time. I will ring Harold and ask him to meet us to show us the exact spot of the old lift shaft base."

After arranging to meet at the reception of the mill; Cathy dressed in the quickest witch time, with a click or her fingers. She still could not work out if it were in her mind or the finger clicking that made the magic work. She took the witch flight route to the mill apartment, where Oskar and Sally met her.

Both had matching grins on their faces. "Where is Clara Jane?" Cathy asked trying the change the conversation, but she knew where it was heading. "She is still with Cynthia, they are together most of the time," replied Oskar, "Tell us about your meeting yesterday, you did not stay around to get us up to date?" Sally was now asking Cathy. "Where are you up to with the young detective?"

Cathy blushing again replied. "I am meeting him with the archaeologist at midday. To look at the site and the see what paperwork is needed to proceed. Apparently, the mill is an historical building. With the crime being committed over a hundred years ago, it must be done properly. It could take a while too," she added.

"Stephen was telling me that you and Adam seemed to get on well," Sally giggled like a teenager. Cathy realised then, that nothing she did would be secret for long in this mill, so she might as well mention the lunch date to them; really is that what she thought it was, or could it just be a working lunch?

"Well, I will let you into a little secret," Cathy smiled, "I am meeting Adam at midday, with the archaeologist, to look at the lift shaft. So they can start the necessary paperwork to get the excavation started. Afterwards, he has asked me out for lunch. So, you can stop your mischievous looks, I am going to be open in this, it could just be a working lunch, so do not get too excited, please."

Sally and Oskar practically high fived each other. "Right, I am going to get my work up to date before I go and meet them. Gran, can you go tell Harold for me, so he can be there as well, as I have no idea where the base of the old lift shaft is."

With that Cathy went into her shop area, switching on the computers and shop lights. She looked around the area and smiles thinking how lucky she was for all this to be happening to her. Her inheritance from her grandmother was turning how to be amazing, if a little magical, with ghosts and murders thrown in.

At 11.30am Harold appeared, with Sally and Oskar. They came into the shop to find her, "won't be a minute," she said, "this new website is generating so many orders these days."

It was very pleasing that other people enjoyed her crystals and oils, just like she did. She was also pleased that she had an organised collection each day with the local courier service. She left the orders in the safe area, and the courier company collected each day at the same time. That was a huge weight of her shoulders. It allowed her the flexibility of processing the orders when she could fit the time in, between one ghost mystery and the next. Once the orders were completed, the trio and cat, walked through the maze of corridors back to reception. As they neared the main entrance, Cathy's stomach did a little flip. She was so nervous; it had been a long time since she felt like this about a lunch date.

As they neared the reception area, Kim came out of the small office to say that Adam and another gent were waiting in the board room. Cathy caught the wink from Kim, before she rushed back to her desk. Did everyone know her business?

Harold led them into the board room, as Cathy shook hands with Adam the magic flowed again. But when she was introduced the Peter, the archaeologist, on shaking his hand there was also a small magic flow too. "Oh no, I hope I don't get this with everyone I shake hands with," she thought to herself.

"Good morning or is its good afternoon?" Adam smiled. "Welcome to you both," Harold replied. As he took charge of the meeting, "Let us make our way towards the site of interest, Stephen is going to meet us there. The two cats, Oskar and Hamish have already been investigating!"

He led the way into the inner workings of the mill, Cathy had not been to this part before, and it felt quite eerie. She had expected the old lift to be near the rickety lift that she herself had been in – once. *"Gosh what must this one has been like then?"* she thought to herself.

On the way to the old shaft site, she saw a few doors that said no entrance. She assumed they must lead to the intriguing cellar area, which were out of bounds to her.

Stephen and Hamish were waiting for them near what looked to be a store cupboard. Adam went straight to Hamish and give him a good stroke and cuddle. "How are you, old man?" he said gently to the old cat.

"Not bad young one," Hamish's deep smooth voice replied. Cathy was surprised as she had not heard Hamish talk before, although she knew Hamish was Oskar's older brother; she never thought about two talking cats.

"Excuse me, I am here too," Oskar prodded Adam, for attention. "Come here your cuddly teddy bear," Adam teased back to Oskar, and proceeded to give him a good scratch too. "These two shouldn't be allowed out together, nothing but mischief, although they do know this mill better than any of us,"

"You should meet their sister, Hannah," laughed Peter the archaeologist, "She is safely at my mothers, I hope."

"Just how many of these siblings are there?" Cathy asked. Oskar, as if reading her mind, "Oh Catherine, you have no idea, we are the original familiar family in Green Valley, one day I will tell you all about my family tree. But for now, we have to concentrate on the job in hand."

Everyone felt justly chastised by the cat's statement and found their way in front of the old lift and the old storage cupboard. Harold produced the key to the cupboard and said, "It hasn't been used for many years, it was the last used years ago, by the old mill cleaner."

He opened the door, and switched the dim light on, all that was inside were the remains of old cleaning equipment; that had been left, alongside years of accumulated dust. It was a considerably basic room, about 10 x 10-foot square.

"So," Peter the archaeologist, "this is where we believe the remains are, from what year?"

"1883," an excited voice shouted out from behind them. An overly excited Clara Jane was with Sally. "I was pushed in 1883, I remember the year well. I was on the third floor when Marty came up beside me and thought it was funny to frighten me. I thought that he was joking and then I saw his face, then he took a proper push and sent me over the empty shaft," her excitement faded away as she remembered the details.

Sally put her arm around her, to comfort her, and to calm her down. "Sorry folks, I couldn't stop her coming down, when she heard what was happening here."

Peter looked over at Clara Jane and immediately realised she was the ghost, whose remains they were about to excavate. "Well, this is not your usual archaeological dig. Cathy when this is all over, I have another dig site, that I would like you to look at if you do not mind. I would like you to have a look, as the ghost whisperer to see if anyone is still around. I guess being in your company allows me to see ghosts too. Right, let us see what we need to do here first before we try to solve other dig site problems."

The room being so small, did not allow everyone inside, but Cathy, Adam and Peter went in first to get a feel of it all. "We will need the papers approved, to let us proceed with the dig. I can sort that out. But I can tell you it will be slow progress; as everything will be done by hand, no machinery will be allowed. Except maybe machinery to break through the concrete on top." Peter continued, "There will only be two other archaeologists allowed on the site, due to the nature of the dig. Everything will have to be recorded piece by piece. There may be clues to date the finds too, that we need to look for. Clara Jane, you will have to make a full statement to the MGA, Adam or Brian can do that. So, we can put everything you remember with the evidence we find." Peter seemed to be in his element and taking charge of the excavation and Adam took a quick glance at Cathy, and the eye contact for both, said let him be the one in charge.

Peter then proceeded to take photographs and measurements. "Cathy, I will process the information and get the necessary papers authorised. I have a couple of members of my team that I would like to work on this dig, it will take time. But will be done as efficiently as possible, under the circumstances. "Clara Jane, it would be easier if you stay away from the area for a while, the other archaeologists do not have our ability to see ghosts, let alone talking cats." With this Oskar and Hamish looked dumbstruck. Continuing, he said "The whole area will be cordoned off, and would it be possible to have a security guard present, to keep prying eyes away, please?"

"Of course, Alf and Eric are the best. I will arrange with them to cover the area. Anything else I can help with? I am on site 24 hours a day. If I am not in the office, I can be found around the mill," Harold told Peter.

After a few more details were noted down, Peter too left, with the witches, wizards, ghost, and the cats.

Adam smiled at Cathy "Shall we head off for lunch now? There is not much more we can do here for now; it is basically in Peters hands till they find anything. Harold, you are ok sorting the security for the site. Clara Jane, we will take your statement when you are ready to sit and talk. Everyone, can we just let the archaeologists do the job now, and please stay away from the area for the time being!"

"Cathy and I will keep everyone up to date with any progress." As Cathy blushed, Adam took her hand and led her back through the mill to the reception. They both felt everyone's eyes on them, even the girls in reception.

Cathy and Adam walked to his car, which was parked in the visitor car park. Peter's car had already disappeared back to the archaeologist offices in town. "Shall we go for lunch then?" Adam asked Cathy, she could tell he was quite nervous too.

"Yes, let's go," she turned around to face him, and as their hands brushed past each other the sparks flew again.

"What is that?" he asked.

"Magic" she smiled at him.

They went in Adams car to a small countryside pub, which overlooked the whole of Green Valley. He had thoughtfully booked a table in the conservatory. As if reading her mind he said, "We are lucky to live in such a wonderful place, aren't we? She smiled in agreement. It really was a beautiful place to be. Adam had ordered the pubs speciality afternoon tea. The food came in picnic hampers and was delicious, finger sandwiches, sausage rolls, spring rolls. Lots of food that they could eat with their fingers, so they could chat at the same time.

"Cathy, I feel I must be honest with you," Adam said quietly. "I was married before and my wife ran off with an extremely rich man. I was never good enough for her and she was always belittling my career and myself. I have not been out with anyone since, as she knocked my confidence for six. So, if I ever appear to be distant or away with the fairies so to speak, just nudge me."

Cathy smiled at Adam and took hold of his hand, the magic just flowed with no sparking this time. "Adam, I am in the same situation, my ex left me because I was not getting the inheritance, he thought I would get. He is currently on a cruise with his latest wife, and good riddance. But without them in our lives, we would not be here today, so let us drink to us being friends and who knows where things may lead. If this magic between us is so special, let us hope it brings us both to better places."

70

"Cheers" they clinked their glasses and smiled, before devouring the rest of the afternoon tea. After a wonderful afternoon Adam dropped Cathy back at the mill apartment, where Kim was waiting for her. "Cathy, don't forget we have the Festival in the Field this weekend!" she shouted to her.

Cathy gave Adam a peck on the cheek to thank him for lunch, and he told her he would be in touch soon. Going back into her shop and apartment Kim followed, "Oh my, he is so dishy." Cathy's smile said a lot and Kim was eager to know what had happened.

Cathy laughed as she went into the apartment, with Kim following. "Oh, my word, I have never been in here before. I had heard rumours that it was the best apartment in the mill, but never thought it would be this spectacular."

Cathy laughed to herself, the first of her new friends to see her apartment. "Do you want a coffee while I tell you the gossip?" she asked Kim. The two young women went to the kitchen and laughed about life in general. Cathy thought at last, her life was getting back to some sort of normality.

Chapter 15

Festival on the Field

Cathy, Kim, and Wendy, all dressed in their finery, arrived at the old sports field. It felt good to be active and normal. No magic allowed, well except from getting ready. Cathy had decided on her flat knee length boots, black jeans, a black sparkly cashmere sweater and leather jacket.

Clara Jane had supervised her outfit, for a ghost from the 1880s, she had quickly caught up modern living. With the help of the TV, which was now her favourite place to be, second only to the crystal workshop. Cathy had got ready at the mill, so that she could meet Kim and Wendy there and get a taxi together. Clara Jane was left in Cathy's apartment, but along with Sally, she was going to visit Cynthia and go through all more her family history.

Clara Jane and Cynthia had spent many hours over the last week going through the memorabilia. Old certificates and even photographs showing Clara Janes siblings, with their grandchildren. Clara Jane was a little sad at first with all that she had missed, from her life being cut short so soon. But now she had a new lease of life and was enjoying learning about her family tree. Even though she was a branch of the same tree from way in the past, she loved hearing Cynthia's tales of the family history. She waved the three women off and wished she could have joined them, but it was not to be – yet. She hoped one day she would learn how to leave the mill again.

The three young women arrived at the Festival in the Field and gave their tickets to the door person, aka ticket collector. Cathy was impressed how the old field had been transformed, and she was sure felt more than a little magic in the air. A large stage was at the far end of the field, and lots of small marquee and tents dotted around the edges of the field.

"Let's go and get our spot near the front," an excited Kim shouted. "We shall claim our patch of grass for the day, near the side of the stage, but with easy access to the wine stall,"

The day comprised of four tribute acts, that the girls were keen to see, ones like the Beatles, The Rolling Stones, a Motown set and finally a Take That tribute, sounded like a fun day ahead of them.

Finding what they thought would be a perfect spot, the three lay out the picnic blanket, and pegged it down, so it would not blow off and finally put their pitch number on, so no one would just pinch their plot. Once the blanket was secure, the three did a tour of the area. Stalls selling wine, beer, wine, sunhats to umbrellas, sweets, and snacks. Everything one would expect at a mini festival. Cathy was interested in a stall selling crystals and incense burners. She had a quick look, nothing to be in competition with her shop, but she still bought yet another amethyst and took a business card "Gillian's Gem Closet" what a sweet name she thought, and a little extra protection never harmed anyone, she thought to herself.

Back at their pitch, the women got ready for the late afternoon entertainment. The first act was named "the Beets" and were fabulous. The whole field was covered in people up dancing and singing along. Cathy looked around and realised she had missed being normal, well she had missed going out since her ex had turned out like he was. The people she had called friends, had been led by his lies, so they had cut her off too. Looking at all the happy faces in the crowd, Cathy was sure she had caught sight of Martin, her ex, in the crowd. *"No, that's impossible he wouldn't have been seen at a place like this,"* she told herself and forgot about it to continue dancing and singing.

The next act was called "The Rolling Bones," that made her smile, Bones, Beets what next, she smiled to herself. She lost herself, dancing, and reminiscing to a few of her favourite tracks. The sun was setting, behind the stage creating a beautiful sunset. *"How lucky am I?"* she smiled to herself, *"to live in such a fabulous place like Green Valley."*

Cathy decided to find the portable toilet block before the act finished and the queue would not be too long. She told Wendy and Kim that she would be back soon, via a kind of sigh language

73

as the music was very loud. "Grab some more wine," giggled Kim using the drinking sign language in return. Cathy headed through the crowd of semi drunken people. "*This could get messy*" she laughed to herself.

Next to the sport field's clubhouse, she spotted the rows of the blue plastic toilet block. "*Nice*" she grimaced, as she joined the queue for the ladies. She was in her own world, still listening to the Rolling Bones, when she felt a tap on her shoulder.

"Well fancy meeting you here, my poor little divorced cousin." Cathy turned to see her cousin Elizabeth stood smugly next to her. She had not seen her since the day at the solicitor's office, a few months ago.

"I heard our grandmother left you nothing in that unit at that old grubby mill," she continued gloating to Cathy. "I have just sold the house and made a tidied sum of money, just over £200.000. I always knew I was the special one."

Cathy did not know how to reply to this distasteful woman, so remained quiet, as her spoilt cousin continued. "Even that unit should have been mine. But when I heard it was empty, I was quite glad that you had got it in the end."

"I am very pleased for you" Cathy replied, "I have never had much, so I will not miss it. The unit is perfect for what I need, so I did not do too bad really."

"Oh, I must go," exclaimed Elizabeth, probably annoyed that Cathy had made her meagre inheritance work for her, "I can't keep my wonderful boyfriend waiting, can I?" and with that she was gone.

Boyfriend, Cathy thought, which is good for her and good luck to him too. From the little she had seen of her obnoxious cousin, poor fella. Well, she was rich, and a good catch and I am poor, Cathy thought. If only she knew what my inheritance had turned out to be.

Finally, after Cathy had done what she had to do, and bought the wine, she attempted to make her way back to her friends.

Friends, she liked having new friends, and this time they were her friends, not their friends, as when she was with Martin. Thinking of him, she felt like she had seen him in the crowd again, with that smug look on his face, must be the drink she thought to herself, he would not be seen dead at an event like this.

Unless it was his ghost she had seen, and she chuckled to herself again. By the time she had fought her way back through the crush and poured the wine into the glasses, Cathy had forgotten all about her cousin and her ex-husband.

The third act on the stage was a Motown music act and everyone in the crowd was up dancing and singing along. Finally, the night ended with a Take That tribute act, and everyone was dancing singing, drinking. There would be few bad heads in the morning, but what a fabulous day everyone was having.

Following the other fellow festival goers, the three of them moved like they were following the pied piper of Green Valley. Orderly queues were formed as over two thousand people staggered out of the sports field.

"How do we get home from here?" Cathy asked, after seeing the queue for the taxis. She felt too drunk to walk to her own cottage and knew witch flight was banned – even if it was possible after so much wine.

"Oh, we did not get chance to tell you, we have moved. It is only a ten-minute walk from here. The solicitor Roger, from the Coven, rang last week to let us know a house came on the market to let. It is your grandmothers old house, that your cousin inherited and sold. It is a fabulous house, with three bedrooms, so you can stay over at ours tonight with us. It is not far from your cottage, but tonight you can be our guest. We also have some wine and snacks waiting for us." The two of them spoke at the same time and seemed more excited than just by the drink and the evening.

"That is a coincidence, I saw my cousin Elizabeth when I went to the toilets. She came up to me and was bragging about how much she had got from the inheritance and how I got nothing. I wonder who bought the house?"

"Roger did not say who the landlord was, just that the house was available for us to rent and at an extremely low rent too," Kim replied. "He knew we wanted something local to the mill. He did all the paperwork and handed us the keys two days ago. With the help of a little magic, the house is now our home."

"So, are you coming along and carrying on the party with us?" asked Wendy. "Then you can tell us both about your boyfriend!"

75

"Absolutely, lead the way," Cathy said, pleased that these two women now treated her so kindly, she did not even mind the teasing.

The three of them started to walk back to the house that was once Sally's and were too busy laughing and singing to notice the man watching them from the corner in the shadows of the social club.

Chapter 16

Back to the Solicitors

Cathy woke up and wondered where she was, then realised she was in her grandmother's old house. She could not ever recall visiting this house; but she had enjoyed staying over with Kim and Wendy. Saying they had only had the keys a few days, they had made the place very homely. Checking her watch, Cathy got up and found the sisters in the kitchen. After her magical breakfast, she begged them for a lift back to the mill as she had left her car at the shop entrance.

Eventually Cathy got back to her own cottage, showered and fresh clothes and strong coffee. Now for a day in front of the tv and chilling, she thought to herself. A wonderful day off and time to recover from the wine induced hangover. It had not helped that they had continued drinking and singing when they got back to the sister's house.

Cathy could hear her phone ringing but were had she left it. She finally found it in her small bag she had taken to the festival the day before.

Grabbing her phone and answering quite breathlessly, "Hello Cathy here," she said.

"Good morning my dearest niece, Uncle John here." She heard her favourite uncle, if the only one she had known for most of her life.

"Hi Uncle John, How's things with you?"

"I am very well Catherine, how are you?"

"I am a little fragile after the festival in the field yesterday, but it was good fun." She replied smiling at the memory. "It was on the old sports field; I went with Wendy and Kim from the mill. I mentioned it last week when we chatted. But so much has happened lately Uncle John, it is hard to keep up with it all."

Laughing, her uncle continued, "yes, I can imagine you being a little fragile. I remember those sorts of events from years gone by. Anyway, the reason I am ringing you on a Sunday morning

77

is, Roger and I need an urgent conversation with you. Today, I can pick you up in say, 20 minutes if you can be ready," the voice was now back to the usual business like.

"Yes, I can be ready, it does sounds very important," Cathy replied, glad that she had showered and changed already.

"See you soon then," her uncle said, "nothing to worry about Catherine, we are all looking out for you." With that he ended the call.

"*Oh no, what now,*" Cathy thought. Well, she would soon find out, he was picking her up in less than 20 minutes.

Cathy was ready, a few minutes before she heard her uncle pip his car horn. She grabbed her bag and phone, running out to meet him in the car. Today he was in the old Aston Martin, Cathy had always loved her uncle's fondness of old cars.

"Oh Cathy, I am so pleased you know your ancestry now. It has been so difficult keeping everything from you over the years." Her Uncle John spoke and seemed so much lighter in himself. "But I had to keep the wishes of your parents, until the time when Sally passed away, and everything came to the open. Right, we best get over to Roger's, he is waiting for us. We may have a problem ahead of us Cathy, but like I said, we are all here for you." With that cryptic message he set off to the solicitor's office.

"Good morning, Mavis," Uncle John greeted the receptionist. "Roger is expecting us," and he marched through the reception to the office at the back of the building.

"Hello, you both," Roger stood up and shook their hand. "Good to see you so soon, Cathy, fabulous work you are doing with the mill ghosts and the Coven members, by the way."

"Right, down to business," Uncle John got the meeting started. "The other day, I got a visit from Martin, your ex-husband. He had heard that your grandmother sadly passed away. He is now, of course, sniffing around for money, as usual."

"Oh no," Cathy was taken aback, "was it really him I thought I saw at the festival yesterday? A couple of times I thought I saw someone with his smug look."

"Probably, yes it would be him." Roger replied, "the problem is, well how do I put this? He seems to believe that you received nothing, and your cousin Elizabeth got all the money."

"Yes, I saw her yesterday too, and she told me she had got in excess of £200,000 for grandma's house." Cathy told them both, "In fact, Kim and Wendy are renting the house, I wonder who bought it then?"

"You bought it Cathy, or your estate bought it. You paid Elizabeth well over the asking price." Roger was telling her, as Cathy looked totally confused.

"The problem we are getting to," replied Uncle John understanding Cathy's confusion. "Is that since your grandmother passed away, your trust fund and her estate have all become yours. Apart from your own cottage, the house of Sally's own and there is other property in the area that she owned. She also left stocks, shares, and money. Roger, Sally, and I have kept up with the investments over the years, for you, Cathy, you are now an incredibly rich woman. Now the problem with that is, the gold-digging ex of yours thinks Elizabeth is the rich one and he is now sticking to her like glue. As she has never met him before, she has no idea he is your ex-husband,"

"We need him to stay far away from you. Yes, I know that will not be a problem on your part. But he is going under the name of Martin Bradshaw now, not Bradbury as when you were married. We have made enquires, since is visit to my house. He is still married to that Gillian woman, who he left you for and went on the cruise with. But on that marriage certificate he is called Martin Bradgate. This man is a serial womaniser and could be a bigamist soon, if you cousin falls for him. We must not acknowledge that he was your ex-husband, until we can work out how we can catch him. We have told Brian and Adam at the MPA, so that they are on the lookout for you too.

"Geez," Cathy exhaled. "I thought I had seen the last of him. What do I do if I come face to face with him?"

"I have Alphin and Alderman, also known as Alf and Eric, the security guys already on the lookout at the mill. They are covering the security of the excavation at the lift shaft," replied Roger. "This is a ring that you must use of you feel in any kind of danger. Press the side here if you need them. I will introduce them to you at the mill once we have finished here."

Uncle John continued, "If you do meet him, you must function as if you have never set eyes on him before, we both know that

79

will be hard for you after all the hurt he caused you. But we think this is how he will want it played out. If you out him in front of your cousin, he may realise you are worth a fortune now and be obsessed with his share."

"Let your cousin feel she is special for once; she has been a nasty woman all her life. This man is just the right medicine for her, I know that sounds harsh, but Cathy, you do not know her. Although I feel you will do in the days to come," Roger finished.

"Well, it will not be hard for me to ignore him and play that I have never seen him before. That man is an idiot and a money leech, he can stick to Elizabeth for all I am concerned, just do not want to see him around here, life had just got extremely exciting for me," Cathy contemplated her ex, not nice man at all.

Grinning, Cathy shyly asked the two men in front of her, "what am I actually worth now?"

The two older men looked at each other and smiled, "A lot of money Cathy, an awful lot, and all of mine to come, when I am no longer here," said Uncle John. "When we get Clara Jane at rest and your ex out of the way, we will all sit down and go through the estate. Now let us let this busy man get on with his work and get you back to the mill. Have you got the ring on Cathy?"

Cathy nodded as she looked down at the purple amethyst ring, with the tiny catch on the side. It was a beautiful ring, and she was sure it had been made especially for her.

Uncle John drove the up to the reception of Riverside Mill, for a Sunday it was quite busy. "Does everyone work on Sundays?" Cathy asked her uncle, "Only when needed," he replied.

He led Cathy through the reception, into the boardroom and Harold and Sally were there waiting for them. Thankfully, they had coffee and cakes ready for them and Cathy dived straight into a strong cup of coffee. "I needed that, with a hangover and the news I just had, I need more coffee and lots of cakes" she laughed.

"Hello, you two," Sally said, "we have been updated on the news of Martin's return, or whatever his real name is. The fact you know now about your estate Cathy, that is a huge relief too. We have worked hard to get everything in place for you, so do not feel bad that we tell you things only when we feel ready. Cathy, do you have the ring?"

"Yes, I have it on my finger," Cathy showed her grandmother, "I put it on for safe keeping, its beautiful, isn't it?" Showing her grandmother, the purple amethyst ring.

"Press the small catch at the side, Cathy," Harold told her, and she did as was told but nothing happened. "There is a knack to it, as we don't want the lads turning up at any time." Sally showed Cathy the way to turn the catch, and almost immediately there was a knock on the boardroom door.

"Come on in," bellowed Harold, he seemed a little excited. The two most enormous men, Cathy had ever seen, walked into the board room.

"This is Alphin, and this is Alderman, normally called Alf and Eric." Harold introduced them to Cathy.

"Mr Harold, Miss Sally, and Mr John, we are pleased to be of service to you. We are incredibly pleased to meet you Miss Cathy, and we will be at you call anytime you need us." Alf was the voice for both.

There was an air of menace about them both, like night club bouncers, but what showed up most, was the amount of loyalty to the people in the boardroom.

The introductions were done and soon everyone was sat around the board room large mahogany table. The coffee and cakes turned into a lunch. "How is the excavation going Cathy," Eric asked her. She was surprised how gentle his voice sounded for such a large man.

"Slowly, there is so much paperwork and red tape that must be produced and procedures to follow. The County Archaeologist is involved now, and we met the other day. With it being an historic building and the event happened over a hundred years ago, it will be a slow excavation.

But I am progressing well, with the help of Cynthia, in the location of Clara Jane's parents and their burial places. But we cannot try to contact them until everything is in place, and we have Clara Janes remains ready for burial."

Alf, sat quietly, in deep thought, "I remember when she went missing, her parents were devasted. Everyone thought she had gone off with that young scallywag, what was he called, Marty or something?"

"You knew them?" Cathy brain was in overdrive, "and his name was Marty? That is a bad coincidence." Cathy remembered Clara Jane saying she had been pushed, but she never took notice of the name of the lad, well she was a beginner to all this magic and ghosts and could not remember everything.

Let us just say, that the two of us, and others that you will eventually meet, are incredibly old," Eric smiled. "I know it seems incredible, as we have told our history a few times, someone once authored a book about the folk lore and giants of Green Valley and included us in it. It was accurate for the time and made proficient reading. But we will tell you all our history once we have reunited Clara Jane and removed the problem of your ex. We will introduce you to our lovely wives, Rimmon and Rowan, and I can see you getting along fine with those two. They are both water nymphs and guard the rivers and lakes around Green Valley." Eric chuckled at the thought of his wife and her sister, and Cathy realised she had made two more new friends for life.

When the impromptu lunch was over, Uncle John took Cathy back to her own house. She needed a bit of down time, after hearing about her ex being in town, not to mention the hangover from yesterday's activities. She needed some oils and meditation, and then sleep to switch off from this roller coaster of a new life.

82

Chapter 17

The Ex-Returns

Cathy fell back into the routine of sleeping at home in her own cottage and witch flighting to the mill in the mornings. She felt it made sense to save fuel when a click of her fingers got her there so quick. She had got used to the dizzy sensation now. Once at the mill she processed her orders and sorted any queries out. This morning when Cathy got to her mill apartment, Clara Jane and Oskar were waiting for her.

"Cathy," Clara Jane, shouted excitedly, as she had just arrived. "The men are back at the old lift shaft; they are going to get started with the dig." No one would have thought it was her remains that were being excavated.

Oskar was a little more serious though, "Cathy there has been a few people at the shop door recently, I dimmed the lights so they couldn't see inside, but I have a bad feeling about them, they have been to the door three times now."

Everyone was nervous about Cathy's ex-husband being in the vicinity, he was a loose cannon.

Cathy said to the others "He will turn up here soon, I feel Elizabeth will be flaunting her new man to me, whilst trying to humiliate me in front of him. But we must remember we do not know him at all. So, let us get to the lift shaft and see what is going on. I hope that Adam will be here, surely the detective would be on site." She was not wasting time thinking about her ex, she had more on her mind than him.

Clara Jane joined in the fun by suggesting the archaeologist was also sexy. Oskar rolled his eyes, if a cat could do that, "I shall go and check on Hamish, and leave you two giggling together." With that and his head held high, Oskar vanished. Cathy had at last, got used to the familiar and others just disappearing and reappearing.

Cathy closed her apartment and with her ghostly companion, she headed towards the old lift shaft in the depth of the mill. Clara

Jane knew the way, as she had been visiting the site most days now, even though she was supposed to stay away.

"Good new Cathy," Peter shouted, "all the paperwork has been cleared. When or if, we find anything, we will be in touch with the coroner. He wants to be informed at every stage. But the guys here are now ready to start the excavation. So, the area needs to be kept clear, no contamination or prying eyes. Screens will be erected around the site."

Adam appeared and smiled at Cathy, "I will let you know how things progress. But everyone not involved will have to leave the area now. Sorry Clara Jane, but I hope you understand the need for this to be done in the best manner possible."

Clara Jane was excited and subdued at the same time, she wanted to stay but knew she could not. So, she let Cathy guide her back to the apartment, to await any further news.

"Can I not stay, it is my remains after all," she begged Cathy.

"Not yet, but it won't be long now, I promise. We will get you and your parents reunited soon. How do you feel about meeting up with your parents, if we can find their ghosts too?" Cathy soothed her with the reply.

"Nervous, excited, I don't know," Clara Jane cried. Cathy would have hugged her if she could, but that was reserved only for the ghost of her grandmother. Cathy could see Clara Jane and her grandma's ghost touch things, but not with Cathy. She did have the gene connection with her grandmother.

"Let's go and sort some crystals," Cathy suggested and tried to change the conversation, she hated seeing Clara Jane upset.

By lunchtime, Cathy had processed the waiting orders, and restocked the shelves. She was feeling incredibly pleased with herself, and she surveyed her small store. Until a knock came to the door, and she felt her stomach turn. Who would be knocking at her door, but she remembered Oskar had said he had seen someone snooping about. She called her grandmother and told her to look after Clara Jane, and to be around as she had an incredibly clever idea who it was waiting on the other side of the door.

She was worried about them seeing the private apartment, but Sally reassured her, that the apartment was covered in magic wards, and no one would see it, unless invited in and the magic let them in.

"Whoever is outside, will only be able to see the shop space and a small bathroom and kitchen at the back of the shop," Sally said. "Go and open the door, after all this is what we had expected. Take a deep breath and don't forget your ring, should you feel in danger."

Cautiously Cathy went to the shop door and unbolted the locks, the first person she saw was her cousin Elizabeth, followed by the person she once thought was her true love.

"Oh, Elizabeth, what a nice surprise, what brings you to my humble unit?" Cathy said, nervous, but certainly not letting them see it. She invited them inside, she turned around to follow them inside, and as just as her grandmother had said, the shop was just that, a shop. A well-stocked small crystal and essential oil shop. Tastefully decorated, but so much was hidden from view. She caught Martin looking at her, a slight blink told her that he wanted her to stay quiet. She knew that look from years of experience. This time she was keeping stum, she was going to see him pay for his actions.

"Oh, you unfortunate old soul," Elizabeth preened. "You did get the short end of the old bags inheritance. A lock up unit with a lot of pebbles, how some people live. I have been so lucky with two parents that looked after me so well. I have never had to get my hands dirty, and now I get the pay out from dear old grannie's house."

Cathy saw that even Martin flinched at her words. Elizabeth, seeing Cathy looking at Martin, quickly did the introductions, "This is MY man, he is called Martin," and to Martin she said, "this is my poor orphaned cousin I was telling you about, when I saw her at the sports field that time. Grannie loved me so much, more than the orphan. Not that I knew much about her, my parents did not mix with riff raff like her and the grandmother. Even this unit should have been mine too."

Cathy was feeling a bit put out with her constant use of orphan and poor. "Well, my dear cousin, the unit could have been yours, but you would have had to be get rid of the rubbish, decorate and stock it. As you have never dirtied your hands with riff raff such as me, I guess it would still be empty. Pleased to meet you,

Martin." She went over to shake hands with him, one to annoy her cousin, but also so he knew she was onto him and his ways of working.

"Is there anything else I can help you with, as I have orders to process?" she asked them.

"Yes, could I use your bathroom," Martin asked in a pathetic voice, oh my word, he was playing the part of the lapdog to Elizabeth. Although she knew he was just being nosey to see what she had in the back room, "Sure, it's just this way," she said leading him to the back of the store.

To her own surprise, it was just as Sally had said, a small toilet with sink in one room and a small kitchen with limited supplies in it for coffee making and a microwave. Cathy smiled to herself, she never ceased to be amazed with her new life and magic.

"I see your looking a bit smug," Martin whispered to Cathy, in his menacing voice. The one that she had heard so much in their brief time together. Yet it did not bother her anymore. "Do not let on you know me to the silly cow of your cousin. This time I will get the money I deserve from your stupid family."

"Wow, you are using my cousin now to get the inheritance you thought I had. My, you are delusional. £200,000 will not get you as far as you want to get. But you have no need to worry. You have heard the way she talks about me, you two are welcome together. Now please excuse me, I must make my petty living by processing the pebbles."

With that Cathy walked out of the small space at the back of her shop, she saw Clara Jane and Sally watching from the shadows, and Oskar came over and rubbed around her ankles, as if he were telling her to calm down, before she said anything more that she would regret.

"Well, a not very pleasant visit, cousin," Elizabeth growled, she seemed jealous that her poor cousin had shown her boyfriend to the bathroom. "We will be on our way, we only called by to say hello and introduce you to MY soon to be fiancé."

"Let me be the first to offer you congratulations, I hope you both will be very happy," Cathy smiled at the pair. Good luck to them both, she thought as she opened the door to let them out.

When she made sure they had left the mill car park, "Grandma, can I ask you a question?" Cathy whispered to Sally. "If Elizabeth is my cousin and her mother was my aunt, and your daughter, how did they become so bitter? The small amount of times I have seen them, they have been incredibly rude to me. Yet we are descendants of you, the most loving woman, I have had the pleasure to meet. I guess my own mother would have grown up like you too."

"Yes, your mother was an incredible woman," Sally looked wistful. "But this is a story for after we have reunited Clara Jane. It is a long-complicated story, Catherine. We will sit down and go through everything once this mess with your ex is sorted completely. Let us go help Clara Jane."

Chapter 18

Coincidences

"Oh my." Cathy slipped to the floor, and the two ghosts rushed over to her, "Are you ok," Sally was concerned, the effect that man had on her granddaughter was awful.

"I am fine, his manners haven't improved, he is still a bully." Cathy sat and let a tear slip down her face. Clara Jane sat down next to her or hovered. "Cathy, what is that man called, he looked and behaved so like Marty that pushed me down the lift shaft?"

"Marty? That man is called Martin, which is a coincidence," Cathy thought aloud, and saw that Clara Jane was shaking in fear again. "Grandma, give Clara a hug will you, I think she has just seen her past flash by her. I have an idea, I did Martin's family history years ago, shall we see if we can find his ancestors, come on Ladies, and Oskar. Time to investigate"

They locked the shop for the day and walked back through the corridor that was now back to its magical normalness. Powering up her laptop, Cathy looked for Martin's family tree.

"Look here it is," she shouted excitedly. "Now I remember, there were different spellings of his name, no wonder is it that he uses various aliases." Cathy showed Clara Jane and Sally the work she had previously done:

Martin was born in Green Valley in 1987, like herself.

His father, also Martin Bradbury, born 1956, in Green Valley.

His grandfather, Martin born in 1934 in Green Valley.

It was looking like a family name, why had she never noticed before, probably because she was in love and believed every word he said.

Great Grandfather Martin Bradburry, (new spelling) was born 1900, and this was interesting, born at Kinders cottages, on the other side of Green Valley.

Great, Great Grandfather Marting Bradburry, born 1867. Born at Riverside mill – could this be the one that Clara Jane knew?

Clara Jane, look at this census return, "*is this the name of his parents and siblings?*"

1881 Census for 4 Riverside Cottage
Marting Bradburry Head Aged 39 mill worker born Green Valley
Marie Bradburry wife Aged 37 domestic duties born Green Valley
Marting son aged 14 mill workers born Green Valley
Fred son aged 11 mill workers born Green Valley
Norman son aged 8   scholar born Green Valley

Clara looked on in amazement that Cathy could find all this information. "Yes, that is the family, we lived at number one."

"He was the great great grandfather of my own ex-husband; badness runs in the family I guess".

Let us see if we can find anything in the newspapers, or his death, let us see how he ended up." Cathy reassured Clara Jane that it was all over, and that she would find out what had happened to him.

I will see if we can find a death certificate first, we know he had a son in 1900, living across the valley. So, we should look after that date. Loading a search on her ancestry website, Cathy did not expect to find the results that she did, prison records, newspaper articles on the local youth that was a thief, not nice reading about this man, he was a persistent thief. Who would have married him and have children?

Cathy printed a few of the newspaper reports and read them to Clara Jane and Sally. Oskar was sat listening, "what does the 1911 census tell us Cathy? He asked, it may show his wife and children.

Searching the census again, she found a family called Bradbury, and a child called Martin, born in 1900 at Kinders cottages, but he was only living with his mother, and of all names she was called Catherine. "This is odd, there is no mention of the Marting we are looking for, maybe he was in prison, or dead!"

Cathy searched again for death certificates between 1900 and 1910, success, she found one in 1904. She paid the subscription and printed it out.

89

Marting Bradburry, born 1867 and died 1904, aged thirty-seven. Accidental death from falling off a ladder as he was attempting a burglary.

Clara Jane started to laugh, "He died by falling, just like I did, that is a good ending. Shame he got so many more years alive than I did." Sally put her arms around Clara Jane. "Well, that closes the question of what happened to him, Cathy is there anything in the newspapers?"

"Let me check, I will search death in Green Valley in 1904, he made the papers again. I feel sorry for the widow and young son, but they were better off without him."

"Oh look, he made headlines, 'Notorious thief gets caught in the act and falls to his death'."

Clara Jane, who had learnt to read with Cynthia, was leaning over her shoulder and reading the article aloud. "He fell thirty feet to his death; sounds like the distance he pushed me. It says he left a widow and young child. Cathy one day can we look more into my family tree, this is so interesting."

"Yes, Clara Jane, we can put all the information Cynthia has, into your tree. We can see what all your siblings did with their lives, and if any other relatives are still alive, like Cynthia. But I need some strong coffee and lunch now, that was some morning." Everyone agreed it was time for a rest, a break from Marty, Martins, and genealogy.

Cathy's phone began to ring, and she looked at the number, it was Adam. It had been a few days since they had been out for lunch. Answering it, she said, "Hi Adam, is everything ok?"

"Yes, I am just ringing to let you know the dig is in progress, but not much to report. They are trying to break through the concrete that was laid down when it was turned into the cleaners cupboard in the 1960s. Peter has brought two other archaeologist and his wife, Susie, she works on the finds table. She is the one that cleans anything that looks of interest, so far, they have found an old sixpence. I am just ringing to see if you would like to go out for dinner this time, I really enjoyed our lunch."

"Yes please, that would be nice," Cathy replied whilst trying to ignore Sally and Clara Jane who were teasing her in the background. "When and where would you like to go?"

"I will ring you when I am at the mill," Adam said, "perhaps we can meet up and decide where to go."

"Sounds good," smiled Cathy. "See you soon."

After the search for Clara Jane's murderers ancestry, Cathy and the two ghosts sat and changed the subject to the archaeological dig taking place.

"I know it's still the first day, but what will they be doing" Clara Jane mentioned the question, everyone had been thinking. They both looked at Cathy to ask what her phone call was about, she laughed and told them about going out again. "Adam told me that the dig as started, but nothing to report back yet."

"Well, I have been a little naughty," Oskar announced. "When I knew your dreadful cousin had left the shop, I went for a little walk. It is most fortunate that I can be invisible at times, the place is all screened off. Alf and Eric are patrolling around the site. There are three people in the lift shaft, I guess the archaeologist, and a massive skip just outside for the rubble to be put in. There is another lady there, she seems to be the one that will inspect anything that is found. Clara Jane, it is happening after all this time. It is officially the dig you have been waiting for.

"The lady on the finds desk, as it is called, is called Susie and she is Peter's wife. She will clean and process anything that is found of interest, Adam just told me that." Cathy told the group.

"This feels so strange and so long in happening. I never dreamt that this day would come at all. It was so lonely in the dark, I screamed for so long, but no one heard me. When I found myself able to leave my body, I stayed so close to the lift shaft to begin with. Like I said before, I did venture to the cottage a couple of times, but when my parents moved on, I was so scared and alone." Clara gently wept and Sally held her close.

"This must be so difficult for you my child, I cannot imagine, I passed away in my bed, peacefully and was buried in the family grave. I chose to remain a ghost, to wait for Catherine, and to then pass on my magic. We can stop this process if you want us to."

"Oh no, not at all, it is just occasionally I feel sad, the last few weeks have been amazing. Living with you and Cathy, meeting Cynthia. I would not give this up at all. It has more than made up

91

for the past. I am so lucky to have seen so much change in the world, for good and bad sadly. The two young men that died in the explosive, two of the banished ghosts. They were so nice at first, we became good friends, till the other two got hold of them. One day, you could bring those two back Cathy. Along with Pearl and Ruby, they were all so nice to me." Clara Jane looked so pleading with Cathy, that she wondered how close she had been with them.

"We will see what happens," Cathy reassured her.

Chapter 19

The Archaeology Dig

As the group were reminiscing over the times of Clara Jane, Cathy's phone rang again, she smiled as she saw the caller ID.

"Hi Adam, that was quick, twice in one day," She laughed. "Yes, I am on site now if you want to meet me in reception. It would be better for now if you come up alone, we do not want to scare anyone, if you know what I mean."

"I am on my way," she told Adam, returning to Clara Jane and Sally. She said, "I am off to reception to meet up with Adam, and I will go and see what is happening at the lift shaft, please, please stay here, even you Oskar. I don't want to mess things up with Adam, just yet."

"Oh, you must go, "Sally agreed, "Clara Jane and I will stay here in the apartment and keep his lordship with us. Hurry along, we want to know what is happening, with the dig and with your romance."

Laughing as she left the apartment, via the secret door, she walked into the maze of corridors. She was now used to the way to the reception area, and soon got there, even if a little breathless. She thought to herself, it had been a while since she had got breathless for a man!

Adam was waiting with Harold in the board room, Cathy was shown in by both Wendy and Kim, both grinning at the prospect of Cathy meeting Adam.

"Hi Cathy," Harold started the conversation, "I hear you had a couple of visitors this morning, news travels fast in this place," he laughed. Adam got up and came over to her, "Are you alright, was he a nuisance?"

"Well, I will admit, it was odd seeing like that, all puppy dog fashion and with my cousin Elizabeth. But since the visit, along with Sally and Clara Jane, we have found out that it was his great, great grandfather that was the one that pushed her into the lift shaft. When she saw him in the shop, she said it was like seeing him again. We had never thought of Marty and Martin being related. Uncanny? We also learnt that he himself, had fallen to his death, during a robbery. It does seem he was a bad one too and left a wife and young son, who were much better off without him. I was so impressed with the enchantment on the shop space, that made it look like just an ordinary lock up unit," she continued. "Of course, he wanted to use the bathroom, and have a nosey. He also threatened me to keep quiet, which I thought was quite menacing. But Elizabeth got jealous, because he was whispering to me, so she took HER boyfriend, soon to be fiancé, out of the shop very swiftly. I thought it quite amusing on her part, that she wanted to keep him away from me. But I do feel he will be back on his own, now he knows where I am working. I do not think he knows my home address. But if he does, I can witch flight over here out of the way. I do not really like the idea of meeting him again, but I feel much safer with this ring on."

Adam put his arm protectively around her waist. "I will do my utmost to bring this chap to justice, Cathy. Shall we have a look at what is happening at the lift shaft. Harold could you please lead the way."

Harold smiled, hoping this young couple would live a happy ever after life. But he knew extremely well, that did not always, happen. His love for Sally had never doubted, even when she met Walter. But he was happy again now, and he saw her every day, even in ghost form.

They arrived at the area were the lift shaft was and were met by a well screened off area.

"Morning Mr Harold, Mr Adam and Miss Cathy," Alf met them. "Have you come to see what's going on?"

"Morning Alf, how is it going, any news yet?" Harold answered.

"Not really sir, it is painstakingly slow. I think they have only got small spoon like things to dig with. But the concrete is all in the skip now. Here, go in through this gap." Alf gestured to a small opening in the side of the screen. They made their way through the gap, surprised at the bright lights that had been set up to illuminate the working area.

"Good morning, great to see you all." Peter was just coming out of the tiny entrance to the lift shaft. "Everyone, this is Cathy,

Harold, and Adam, that we have been talking about. Susie, come over here, this is Cathy, the ghost whisperer, that I have been talking about." A young lady came over and shook Cathy's hand. "So pleased to meet you at last, Peter has been raving about you. But watch him, he will have you at every site we have ever worked on. To see if you can detect any more ghosts, and find out any more information for him." She laughed, as her husband put his arm around her and kissed her, probably to shut her up.

The two other archaeologist in the small area came out and were introduced as David and Nigel, brothers that worked together, for Peter. "Come look at this," they told everyone, "We may have found something."

"Take a photo," Susie said, "we can't all go and contaminate the site."

"Good idea," agreed David. They all congregated around David's phone, until Susie suggested sending it to the laptop, where everyone could see it better. The excitement soon stopped when everyone realised it was a coin, but when excavated it was from the 1960's.

"That must have been dropped, when the lift shaft was filled in to make the cleaners cupboard," Harold added. "But it's a start in the right direction."

The two brothers got back to work, tiny scrapers pulling the soil, back inch by inch. The spoil was meticulously measured and checked before being put into the skip. Nigel laughed and said "This will take days to get down, but we will be here working away. You will soon hear if we find anything. The first sign of anything significant and you will be told."

Nigel and David looked the part of archaeologists, with their bushy beards and geeky looks. They had to remove the dirt, inch by inch. Each particle would be studied, and hopefully, Clara Janes remains would be uncovered. Cathy just knew that this was the place.

After a few more pleasantries, the trio made their way back to reception. Harold left them to go check on his staff. Cathy and Adam walked outside and to the car park, where Adam had left his car.

"Well Cathy, things are progressing with the excavation, we should hear more in a couple of days. Can I ask, how are you feeling with the return of your ex-husband?"

"I am ok, he is the same bully as he always was. I feel for Elizabeth, being with him £200,000 will not go far. But she is besotted, as she ever had a boyfriend before, do you know?"

"No idea to be honest, as they have never appeared on the paranormal lists, they have just lived their normal lives. I do know she lives in the converted garage at her parents' house. She has been spoilt by her father, but he is an awkward man, business circles say they do not like dealing with him."

"What business is he in? I know nothing about them," Cathy asked.

"Shall we go grab a coffee?" Adam said, leading her towards the small café they had been in before.

Continuing the conversation when they had ordered their coffees, Adam continued, "I don't know much about your aunt and uncle, I can investigate them, through work. It is strange that both you and your grandma have magical powers, and I assume your mother had too. So why wouldn't your aunt and Elizabeth? I can see what I can find, unofficially, if you want to know."

"Are you sure it would be ok, I don't want to get you in trouble," Cathy was cautious, she wanted to know her family background, but something felt a little off.

"Leave it with me, lets enjoy our coffee and plan out night out," Adam, took her hand and smiled, and she knew it would be alright. "Would you like to come to my place for dinner one night and sample my cooking. It is not the best, but we can talk more openly than in a restaurant?"

Cathy agreed it would be lovely to see his house, and sample to cuisine. She teased him by saying, "if your food isn't up to standard, I could magic us our favourite foods, as my magic is getting better now."

Adam replied, "how did you think I was going to prepare food? You know something Cathy, it is so good to have someone like me, someone that understands magic."

Chapter 20

The Workhouse and Church Records

After saying goodbye to Adam, Cathy made her way back to her apartment. Although it was late afternoon, she wanted to continue the research on Clara Jane's parents. She wanted to be organised for the next step, for when the excavations were complete.

Starting with the Green Valley workhouse. She knew nothing was left of the original buildings; they were now exclusive apartments. The old workhouse had stood on one of the highest hill tops, overlooking the whole of the Green Valley. The old photographs showed it was a three-story long building and farmland.

Researching the workhouse, Cathy expected it to be like the tale of Oliver Twist, by Charles Dickens, dark, cruel, and only gruel to eat. But the newspaper archives told her a different story for the workhouse at Green Valley.

Articles in the newspapers told of the guardians' meetings and reported the Christmas parties held at the workhouse for the inmates. Summer trips and visits from local school children. One article in the local history society had a report by a lady, who had known the daughter of the last workhouse master, which talked about the people that lived there. How they ladies were all dressed in pinafore type uniforms, and that the children all played out together. This article was from about 1930, when the workhouse changed its name to the fever hospital.

The workhouse, moved to the high hilltop site, around 1841 and was in use of one kind or another until the 1960s, when it was left and became derelict. At the time of Betty and John Holroyd's stay, the master was a man called John Wood and his wife Emma, they ran the workhouse from about 1881 to 1900. Cathy knew she would have to go and look at the old site but needed to ask her grandmother about all the other ghosts that could be there, and how she could concentrate only on the ones that she wanted.

The church records were easier to find, as Cathy already had the death certificates of Clara Jane's parents, so knew the dates of their death. Church online records showed the burial dates and burial plot of them both. So, a trip to the cemetery was in store too, but the church was only half a mile or so from the remains of the workhouse.

Again, Cathy flinched at the number of ghosts that may be on the lookout for a ghost whisperer. The main church of Green Valley was first built in the 12th century, with additions built on over the years there were four graveyards, the oldest behind the church, one in front of the church. Another one at the top of the road leading to the church, and a new modern one next to this one. Looking at the plans for the grave layout, Cathy thought that the grave of Clara Jane's ancestor was in the cemetery in front of the church. Printing off the church cemetery plan, Cathy started to label the grave rows to help her find the area she was looking for.

She felt the cold breeze and realised that Sally was on her way. "What are you doing at this hour?

Cathy looked at the time and was surprised it was going up to ten o'clock. "I was researching the workhouse and church yard, I must have lost track of time, I have found a few interesting things, gran," Cathy replied, showing her the work, she had done.

"I do have a question though, grandma," Cathy did not quite know how to approach the subject. "If I am a ghost whisperer, how will I manage to contact the right ghosts? I am scared I will be overwhelmed and fail Clara Jane."

"That is a good question," Sally answered, "I will ask the other members from the Coven, what they think. I know we will have to have a few more lessons and you must consult the grimoire. Now I suggest you have some food and stay here tonight. We do not want your ex visiting your house. I am sure Madam will have shown him your little hovel." She smirked as she said the last bit. "Did you hear what she called me today!! The young stubborn fool, £200,000 later and she still insults me." With that, Sally conjured up some of Cathy's favourite food, and teasingly asked how Adam was, whilst watching Cathy blush. Cathy updated her grandmother on the dig, the coffee, and the next date.

"What magical beings are Stephen, Brian and Adam, Grandma?" Cathy asked, she had not like to ask Adam himself, although she agreed, it was good to know he was magical too. Although I guess if you are a detective with the magical police academy, you have some paranormal being inside.

"They are all wizards Cathy, and a good family. You do make the perfect couple." Her grandma waved her to her bedroom, "Get some sleep young lady, it is going to be a busy, if not a bumpy road for a few days ahead for you. If you don't want to meet every ghost lingering at the graveyard."

With that Cathy gave in, and went to bed, finding Oskar flat out across the bed. "Shift over Fluffy," she laughed, calling by his old name on purpose to annoy him, as she climbed in.

After a few normal days, and more researching Cathy got the call she had been waiting for. Adam had rung and told her to meet him in reception, the archaeologist think they may have found what we are all looking for.

"Sally, Clara Jane, Oskar," she shouted her grandmother, where are you all, we need to get moving."

Out of nowhere the two ghosts and the familiar appeared. "The archaeologists have found something, and I must go meet Adam at reception. Clara Jane, will you be all right?" Well, it was not everyday archaeologists excavated your own remains.

"I am fine, I think. It feels weird. I have been in ghost form for so long now, and the past few months have been more than I could ever ask for. Cathy, you go along and meet Adam, we can come along when its ready for us." Clara Jane and Sally looked at each other and sent Cathy off to meet Adam.

As quick as she could, without running, Cathy made it to reception. Adam was waiting and talking to Peter, the County Archaeologist. "Hi Cathy," they both said.

"We have come across the remains," Peter told her. "They are in a bad condition after all this time, and they have been squashed down with the weight of the soil. But we are taking them out bone by bone and laying her out on the finds table. We have taken photographs for our records. Unfortunate thing still has remains of her old grey smock and shoes. She must have been crouched in the corner, with what is looking like a badly broken leg. Unfortunate thing, to think of the horrors she must have suffered after she fell. The time after falling to dying, we won't be able to tell, with the state of the remains. But we will be able to get a DNA match, to confirm the remains, if that would be possible. Do you know anyone?"

"Oh yes, Cynthia is a descendant of Clara Janes youngest brother, that would work, wouldn't it? I can ask her if you want." Cathy was sad thinking of the poor child all alone, after her fall. How has Clara Jane managed to overcome all that.

Adam answered her, "I will have to do it via the coroner's office Cathy. That is where the remains will go to be signed off, for the burial. If you could give me her details"

"Shall we make our way to the site," Peter led the way. Cathy was unsure about seeing the remains, as she had not seen many dead bodies, let alone a skeleton. Sensing her discomfort, Adam took her hand and told her, "Its ok Cathy, you won't think of the remains as Clara Jane, just think of it as just some old bones."

Once Cathy got to see Susie, at the finds table, she knew what they meant about the bones, all there was, were a small pile of remains. But she was only fourteen and a tiny person anyway.

"Hi Cathy," Susie smiles, "Look at these tiny shoes we have found, how delicate they are, saying she was a mill girl. Maybe she was in the mill at the wrong time and not working, maybe in her Sunday best?"

The tiny leather, hand stitched shoes looked like they had seen a lot of wear, before being sent into the lift shaft. "Have you any remains of her smock?" Cathy asked.

"Tiny fragments, the years have not been good to the material. There is an old penny too, dated 1883 – I wonder if it was put down with her, as a sort of afterthought."

Susie explained what everything was, and what the bones where, they had near a full skeleton, of a small 14 -year-old mill worker, from 140 years ago.

"It is in a lot better condition that we expected. After all this time, we weren't sure we would find anything at all," Peter joined in the conversation.

David and Nigel were still digging in the small space, every now and again they stopped and took photographs recording everything they uncovered.

"I had better get back to Clara Jane and let her know what is happening. She is eager to know. It is strange that this is her body, and yet, her lifelike ghost is just down the other end of the mill.

Shyly, she asked Adam if he would like to go back with her, he had invited her to his place, so now was time for to introduce her to her magic apartment too. Rather than go through the mill, they took the scenic route, along the riverside, and back to the shop entrance.

Although she had not actually opened the shop for any customers yet. Cathy now referred to this area as the shop, and the Temple room, as the workroom. As they walked along, she wondered how the magic apartment would appear to Adam. She knew he was a wizard from an old family of wizards, but she had not really taken anyone back that was becoming special to her feelings.

Chapter 21

The Ex meets Alf and Eric

As they rounded the corner, by the visitors car park, Cathy spotted an old car, that looked way to familiar. "Adam, can we just go check that car out, the one in the corner of the car park, please," she asked him, as she headed towards the car.

"Do you know this car, "Adam asked her, taking out his phone as if to check the registration.

"Yes, I do, it is Martin's, my ex, it is his old car. He had been driving a new BMW, but this one was his pride and joy for some reason. What is it doing parked here?"

"The car is registered to a Martin Bradshaw, wasn't he Bradbury when with you? I bet he is waiting at your lockup for you. You did say you felt that he would be back. Let's get Alf and Eric round here, just for back up. I have a feeling he is not here for pleasantries, Cathy." Adam seemed a little concerned.

"Whatever he is up to, we must remember not to do anything that will jeopardise the case, that the police are building against him. Maybe you go round to the unit, and the lads and I will just stay out of sight. Do you have your ring on?"

"Yes, I don't take the ring off these days," Cathy showed him. "Time for you to see if it works, best they meet us here in the car park, then we can plan the way ahead." Adam told her.

Nervously Cathy twisted the catch on the ring, and before she could blink, the two giants were stood next to her. Adam filled them in on the fact that Cathy's no-good ex was waiting for her at the lock up shop, round the side of the mill. That he wanted Cathy to go alone to see what he wanted, and if any trouble, Adam. Alf and Eric would step in.

The four of them walked along the riverside pathway, and then took the path to the rear of the mill. Martin was nowhere in sight. But Alf spotted that the shutter to the unit was open, and the door looked to be ajar. "This doesn't look good Miss Cathy," he said. "It looks like he has broken into your shop."

"That is not good, let me go in and see. The last time he was in, he was being very nosey. Funnily enough, I felt he would be back. I am glad you three are with me." With that Cathy walked over to her lock up shop to survey the damage done to the door and shutter.

"Is anyone inside?" she shouted nervously, as the three men crept by the side of the mill wall. "Come on out anyone that is inside," She shouted again, slowly opening the door.

"Oh, come on in Catherine," the old smug voice called back at her, "You know it is me, locksmith extraordinaire."

Cathy went into the shop and was relieved to see it was just the shop she could see. "What brings you here, to break into my unit? And where is my cousin, your wonderful girlfriend. I bet she doesn't even know you are here, does she?"

"I have been waiting ages for you, and it got cold, so I thought it best to wait inside for you, nice little place you have here Catherine." Calling her the full Sunday name was annoying Cathy more than him being there. "What is it you want from me?" she snapped back at him.

That is no way to greet your loving husband, Catherine." He had that same smug look on his face, she wished she could knock it off. "I came to see how you are doing, nice little set up you have. Shame you do not have much cash lying around, I could only find this tin with £600.00 in it. Do you have anymore, or will this have to do?"

"You break into my unit, both the shutter and door, and then look for money, you are no more than a petty thief. I sell online, I do not sell for cash, the money in the tin, is for emergencies only."

"Oh, after all this time, I did not break in Cathy, you gave me your keys on the last visit here, when I was with my fiancée. You had a set hung up in the tiny kitchen. I just helped myself to them. Anyway, I need some more money, as you delightful cousin is insisting, I pay my own way, and you know dear Cathy, I have never done that. So, if you could just lend me the money from your inheritance, I will be on my way."

"This is my inheritance, Martin, what you see is what you get, always has been with me, remember?"

"Now, I know that you got some cash, as Elizabeth told me you had. She told me you got at least £20,000 from the will of your grandmother."

"Good grief, the woman is even telling lies about me now, lies to you. You saw the pity in her face when you both visited the other week. How come I am suddenly worth £20,000?"

"Your lying Cathy, I can tell. Now give me the money and I will leave you alone." Martin was beginning to get annoyed; his rich fiancée was telling him lies already, had she cottoned on to him? Was she setting him up or did she know about him and Cathy?

"I can assure you Martin, when we divorced and sold our house, you left with the lions share. I use my share to update this business and rent a small cottage out of town." She added the last bit, to throw him off her small cottage in the village. "Take the £600.00 you found and leave the keys on the counter. Leave this place and never come back."

"Oh Catherine, how could you lie to me, your cousin Elizabeth is twice the woman you are! We both know you have more money squirrelled away. The bank accounts for the business look interesting, yes, I had a quick look on your computer whilst waiting for you."

He moved over towards her and took her arm, "Now you know Catherine, I still deserve half of any share you got. After all, I was your husband for better or worse. Now this is my bank details, and you can transfer me the money across – now".

Cathy felt very intimidated now, although she knew the three men were outside, she knew she had to play along for now. He could not have seen her bank account, as they were done on a separate device, that he would never find, deep in the Temple room of the apartment. "How much do you think I have, Martin. Which bank account did you manage to log into?

"Just transfer the £20,000 for goodness sake Cathy, I haven't got all day." His grip on her arm began to hurt.

"I will not transfer any of my hard-earned money to you, never" she now cried out, she thought he might break her arm now.

"What is pretty Miss Catherine going to do about it now?" his voice took on a sinister tone. "You have never lived up to what you first told me you were. Trustee to a fortune, you told me, all those years ago."

"I never, I told you my parents died young, they had no money to leave me. My uncle took me in, that was the truth of my background and well you know it. If I had been rich, I guess you would have taken the money and run off into the sunset, wouldn't you? But no, I did not have any money, now or then, and you still went off into the sunset. Should I tell Elizabeth about our marriage?"

With that last comment from Cathy, Martin saw red. "You will not tell that cow about us, she has the money you were supposed to have, it will all be money one day."

"£200,000 will not keep you in the lifestyle you imagine yourself in Martin, or will it help you on the next step to the wealthy widow?" Cathy snarled back at him.

He twisted her arm so much, she felt something snap and cried out in pain, as he flung her across the floor of the shop.

At the same time, Adam, Eric, and Alf just sauntered into the shop, so calmly, as if nothing was going on at all.

"Oh Miss Cathy, are you ok, what are you doing on the floor," Alf came over to her. She noticed that Eric was stood blocking the door, so Martin could not escape.

Adam helped Cathy up and looked at the purple fingerprints on the wrist, where Martin had held her tight. "That looks nasty Cathy, how has this happened, doesn't look like a fall to me".

"Oh, she fell over, she was fetching some crystals for me to look at." Martin stumbled his excuse growing less with every sentence.

"I love Miss Cathy's crystals," Alf, joined in, "Which ones were you looking for, I love the different powers each crystal has, which is your favourite Sir?"

Martin was taken aback, he thought these men were odd when they walked in the shop, who on earth would like this rubbish of different coloured pebbles."

"Err the purple ones, that's the one." He mumbled back.

"Sounds to me, that is not why you were here at all," Adam joined in. Cathy thought they were enjoying this, her arm hurt, but she knew it was not broken, but Martin did not know that.

"Officer," Cathy called Adam. "When I arrived at my unit, the shutter and door were open, this man had come into my lock up. He said he I had given him the spare keys when he visited recently with my cousin Elizabeth. But I know that there are no spare keys left in the lock up. Why would I leave them inside the lockup? If I were locked out, they would be useless."

Martin turned a slight shade of grey at the name of Officer. He turned to leave but saw Eric filling the entire doorway. "This lock has been broken officer." Eric joined in the fun too. Cathy tried not to smile, as her three good friends were making her ex-husbands life so amazingly difficult.

"I suppose, you had better accompany us to the station, sorry I didn't catch your name?" Adam, in his most official voice asked.

"Police station, no you have it all wrong, Cathy is an old friend, I was just visiting her. Please this is all a misunderstanding," he was now pleading. He could see his future with Elizabeth, and her money, slipping away.

"I, have a compromise, return the money you have stolen, and leave these premises at once. Leave in the old Celica and never set foot on the whole mill estate ever again. Everything that has happened here today, has been recorded on CCTV, even parking your car in the car park. To you picking the lock on the shutters and door. CCTV in the shop as recorded your every move before I got here and after. I have enough information to send your Elizabeth away from you for good, let alone the police. Now leave. The two men will escort you to your car." Cathy was quite the dominant now.

Martin looked confused, "How did you know about the car?"

"You were never that bright Martin; the old Celica is parked in the visitor car park. We followed your movements, as we do with anyone acting suspiciously on the premised," Cathy laughed.

"Now run along let a good lapdog, back to Elizabeth, tell her your money is in bonds, and takes thirty days to cash in, she will buy that, you're definitely two of a kind."

Cathy turned her back on Martin, as Eric and Alf, led him out of the shop. Adam turned to her and asked "are you ok?"

"Actually, I feel amazing, I felt so good telling the snivelling little rat what to do."

Alf and Eric soon returned, "he has gone now, he kept saying he had been set up," giggle Eric. She loved these two giants of men. "Let's meet up later and all have some food," Cathy suggested.

"Excellent idea, catch you both later," they both agreed and set off back to the excavation site, to continue their work.

"Adam, close your eyes a minute, I need the shop locked and returned to normal. Looking confused, he did as he was told.

Cathy pulled the shutter down, locked the door magically for now. She turned to see her shop and corridor to the apartment visible.

"This way," as she took Adams hand and led her to the apartment. Opening his eyes, Adam could not take in the transformation, "What just happened" he asked her.

"Adam, its magic again. You do not use your magic much, but for this apartment to let you in, it says you too have incredible skills just waiting to be unbound."

As they entered the lounge of the apartment, Sally and Clara Jane were waiting. Adam found he could see them just as easy as Cathy could.

"Cathy, oh how are you, that man is a bad man," Clara Jane was calling. "Why did you just let him go?"

"It is complicated Clara Jane, when we have all the information on him, he will be put away for an awfully long time. Where you both watching?"

"Yes, we heard the commotion of the shutter and lock of the door, and thought it was Cathy coming back to tell us what had happened, and then we saw him breaking in," Sally explained. "Clara Jane has been practising leaving the building, in preparation for her visit to meet her parents. We saw that Adam was with you, so came back in the shop to make sure it was non magical. He did not notice the cold breeze around him. But he is awful, Cathy, you are so much better off without him."

"I know, but he needs to be caught out for more than bullying and breaking and entering. Adam here, along with Roger is making a full case against him, so that's why we had to just scare him off today. Anyway, the good news is that Clara Janes remains have been found, you poor child, curled up like that for so long. But tell me, was it a Sunday when you were in the mill with Marty? Cathy asked Clara Jane.

"Why do you ask?" Clara Jane said quietly.

"You had your Sunday best outfit on didn't you, there is no way those shoes were the work shoes, so delicate and dainty" Cathy told her, they have found your clothes too, although everything is in a bad way, with the lift shaft being closed soon after you fell, your body was covered over, and then in the 1960s, a concrete floor was put on top of the soil to make the cleaning cupboard."

"Yes, we had been to Sunday School. Marty was teasing me and said he wanted to go into the mill while no one was in. We wanted to see what it was like when the weaving room was empty and quiet. We worked five and half days a week, it was just curiosity. We knew the security guard took a break mid-afternoon, so we went in through one of the side doors. We went to the top floor, it's the one I worked on. He told me to look how deep the lift space was. It was only for one of those pulley lifts to take stuff one floor to another, but never really got used.

I looked down the dark void, and he pushed me. I heard him laughing, just the laugh like your ex-husband laughed, sinister. I screamed for help, and I hurt my leg. It went quiet, then I felt some pennies throwing down at me, he told me it was good luck for my next journey. I didn't know what he meant at the time, but I think back in the day, people put coins on the eyes of the dead. I heard him outside the lift door, where I had landed, but then I heard him walking away whistling to himself. I cried, I screamed, I died."

Everyone was silent, what a dreadful ending to such a short life. "Once the coroner has matched the remains, and taken a DNA swab from Cynthia, to help match the remains to you, we can release the remains for burial." Adam joined in the conversation.

"Yes, Clara Jane, are you ready to meet your parents, and I feel you need to dress yourself in a similar Sunday best, something they would remember you wearing," Cathy gently told her.

"I will need to visit the site of the old workhouse, and churchyard soon. I need to try to find Clara Janes parents. I have been learning how to block the other ghosts out, although I know it will not be easy. Do you think anyone else needs to come with me?"

"We can discuss this another time Cathy. Clara Jane and I will go and visit Cynthia and Betty, and leave you two in peace for a while. It has been a busy day. Adam, how long do you think it will be before the remains are released?" Sally replied.

"Once the DNA results are back and the coroner signs everything off, a week or so. Will that give you time to contact Clara Jane's parents Cathy? I know Cynthia did the DNA swab the other day, so that shouldn't take long." Adam replied, "any chance of a coffee Cathy?"

With that, the two ghosts disappeared, and Cathy and Adam were left alone, in the enchanted mill apartment. "Do you want a quick look around?" she asked him, wondering if the Temple room would open or not – it didn't. But she knew it would do one day soon, she could feel it in the warmth of the magic coming from Adam.

Chapter 22

Clara Jane's Parents

Cathy woke the following morning, smiling at herself, she had a lovely evening with Adam, and reluctantly they said goodnight, after arranging dinner at his house the following weekend.

She had stayed at the mill, it was too late to go back to the own cottage, she was spending more time at the mill these days, but it felt much safer with her ex-husband around, she did not trust her cousin to not tell him where she lived, now he was banned from the mill.

Cathy knew her next job would be to try to find Clara Janes parents. She would begin this part of the quest at the old workhouse site but didn't feel like going alone. She called for Sally, and almost immediately her ghost appeared.

"Gran, I think I am ready to try a visit to the site of the old workhouse, but who will come with me? I have been practising how to block out unwanted ghost, but still feel a little uneasy until I have actually tried it for real."

Sally replied, looking concerned was Cathy ready for this yet? "I think it would be good if Desdemona, Betty, and Harold went with you to start. Four of you in one car for ease, and I will be there, of course, as I am not confined to the mill. If we need to get away quick, so be it, and in that case, we will consult the Coven members. When do you want to try?"

Cathy thought about it and said, "Well the excavation is nearly complete, and the coroner has been informed. Cynthia's DNA sample has been with the lab a while, so everything is falling into place. I guess the sooner the better, to get the next part of the plan started. I think Clara Jane needs to stay at the mill to start with, until we find her parents ghosts, or remains. They may have already passed over. Shall we have a visit in the next few days if everyone can make it, what about Cynthia, she is there relative too?"

"Good, I will go and find Dessi and Betty, and yes, I had better ask Cynthia too, like you said, she is family. Shall we aim for tomorrow lunch time, give us a few hours to look around, and if anyone sees us from the new apartments that are now there, we can say we are local historians!" Sally disappeared as quick as she had arrived.

Cathy made herself some breakfast, how she had managed without magic, seriously worried her nowadays, it was so useful for so many things. She turned her music on and got her laptop out to check any online crystal orders, whilst she ate her breakfast. A few hectic days ahead of her she thought. She decided to create a new piece of crystal jewellery, to add a little extra protection for herself. The idea of contacting Clara Jane's deceased parents filled her with nervousness and excitement. Any extra protection she could provide would make her feel better, or at least she thought. Which should she use, she thought she would create a necklace and bracelet.

- Clear Quartz, to deflect any negativity.
- Black Tourmaline for grounding and it is a strong and powerful protection stone.
- Amethyst, her favourite, is rich and healing stone, especially good if lots of people are around, (which she hoped didn't happen,) it also helps to provide protection from negative energies.
- Pyrite which has a strong energy and reach, making it one of the ideal crystals for protection.
- Turquoise is well known in folkloric history throughout many cultures. It was used as a conduit to speak with the spirit world, and as a talisman to guard burial sites,

She thought these crystals would give her confidence and maybe help her connect with the ghosts. She set about making the jewellery, and soon became absorbed in her work. A few hours later when she was satisfied with her work, she looked up to see Clara Jane watching her.

"How long have you been watching?" she laughed. "Just after you started making the bracelet. I was listening to you talking to yourself about the properties of each different stone. I kept quiet as I didn't want to disturb you. But it is the first time I have seen you create anything. You are amazing Cathy. I wish I could

111

create like you do. I can touch things much better now. Can you teach me Cathy?" Clara Jane pleaded.

"I am going to the old workhouse site tomorrow, Clara Jane, to see if I can contact your parents. Are you ok with that?" Cathy did not want to get Clara Janes hopes up if she would be leaving them soon when she passed over with her parents.

"Oh yes, it will be so good to see them again," and just like that, she was back to the young child again. Cathy felt so much for this young girl, here she was living the life of a teenage ghost in the 21st century, yet she had died in the 19th century, she was going to miss her. But that was the quest she had been set, to reunite her with her parents.

"So do you like the matching set, I have just made?" Cathy asked Clara. "Would you like to try it for yourself?"

"Can I? Yes please." An excited child was just about to make her own bracelet. "What colour is your favourite Clara Jane?" Cathy asked. "The yellow ones please"

"The yellow is called citrine, helps clear the negativity from your mind, it helps to bring positive energy and reduce sadness when worn. Excellent choice. Now let us find you a variety of small stones and a bracelet length. You will have to make it, because if I do, I will not be able to pass it to you. The human ghost touch, is not there between us yet."

Over the next hour or so, Clara Jane and Cathy attempted to make another bracelet, not an easy thing with one person being a ghost. But it was fun whilst they worked together. Cathy gave instructions and eventually Clara Jane could get the small beads threaded onto the elastic bracelet string. Cathy felt that this would be what a younger sister would be like. Clara Jane was beside herself as she slipped the completed bracelet on her tiny wrist. A bit of magic helped the process too!

So impressed with herself, she quickly excused herself and went to show Cynthia her had work. Cathy smiled fondly about the young girl. Her life cut short and now she was kind of living again and is certainly loved by everyone in the mill.

Now Cathy thought she had better have a look again at her grimoire and prepare for tomorrow's task at the old workhouse place.

Another few hours with her grimoire, setting her intent and finding protection spells for herself, from unwanted ghosts, Cathy finally decided to stop for the day.

Tomorrow was going to be busy, Sally had returned to say everyone was on board, for 1200 noon, to leave the mill. Clara Jane was going to stay with Stephen, Hamish, and Oskar, while they were out. It was felt she needed to be with someone, so she wouldn't try to leave the mill on her own.

She couldn't decide whether to stay at the mill, or witch flight back to her own cottage. She decided that it was probably for the best she stayed at the mill. It had been very quiet on the ex-husband front, and although she liked it that way, it also made niggling thoughts as what he was up to now. She hoped the run in with Alf and Eric would scare him off, but she knew him only too well. Sleep did not come easy for Cathy that night. Too many things whirling around in her mind.

She got up early and went to her shop, the orders were plentiful these days, and although she was pleased about it, she felt she didn't show the business enough time these days, with her magic taking over. *"Oh, to have an assistant,"* she thought to herself, again.

At midday, on the dot. A knock came to her door, and the four witches were waiting for her. Cynthia looked like she was in her Sunday Best outfit, but then she was about to go on a ghost hunt for her ancestors.

Sally joined them and seemed rather excited too. "It is so good to be able to go on a quest again. We have all been so bored for years because nothing magical has happened in the area. My own death brought you too us Cathy, and we are all so delighted. Let's get the show on the road, is that the correct saying?"

They all left the apartment and piled into Harold's old car. Cathy loved the way these eccentric men all had many cars to suit their needs. Today was an old Jaguar, that fitted the five of them I comfortable. Of course, Sally would meet them at the workhouse site.

Driving along the back roads of Green Valley, Cathy knew where the name had come from. High up on the hillside, above the small town, you could make out the route that the glacier took

113

all those thousands of years before. A long valley between the hills on each side. Green Valley was a perfect name.

As they passed the old church, Harold said he was not going to drive direct round by the church, as he did not want the ghosts from the graveyards mixing with the workhouse, just yet. So, at the crossroads, with the church directly in front, Harold took a right turn and went even higher up into the cloudless sky.

"We will reach the old place just around a few more bends," he told Cathy as they drove along the single-track road. She felt like they were driving up and up into the heavens. After a final turn, they came into view of the modern single-story building, that was all that was left of the three-story workhouse and farm.

Harold pulled the car over and told the others to stay in the car for now. He walked over to the first of the apartments and knocked on the door. It turned out that Harold knew the owner of the complex and had forewarned him of our visit, to Cathy's relief. She had been worried about trespassing and stuffy people that didn't want disturbing,

Walking back over to the car, Harold was joined by Sally and another gent, that even looked like he could be Harold's brother. "Ladies, I would like to introduce my cousin Gilbert to you, I didn't let on about him living here, as we didn't really know if this day would come or not."

After the introductions were taken care of, Gilbert led Cathy to the old entrance to the workhouse. "I have always been fascinated with this place," he told her. I never dreamed we would try to contact anyone from so long ago, but I am game if you are." He laughed and Cathy found herself with another excited old wizard.

"The workhouse was first on this site around 1841. It only had ten sets of Matrons and Masters in all the time it was in use." He told her the history of the place, although she had found most of it out a lot herself, with her research.

"It used to be a three-storey building, pretty bleak as you can imagine so far above the township of Green Valley. Not a place you wanted to end up in, I wouldn't have thought. Around the time of Clara Janes parents time here, there would have been a working farm. The children if well enough would have gone to the local school, dressed in their poor house uniform of a dark

114

grey pinafore. Now where do you want to look first. I have a map of the old place and a one of now, so we can try to recreate the main hall that the inmates, (oh I don't like that term), would have had their meals together. Shall we try that area first?"

Cathy was surprised at his knowledge, and preparation work, she had not thought of the layout at all. She also did not like the term inmates but was pleased the poor children got some schooling at least.

The group of witches, wizards and ghost headed towards an area in one of the fields near the new buildings.

"This is where I feel the main hall of the workhouse would be," announced Gilbert. "Good thing old chap," answered Harold. Cathy could see how these two would have been great characters in their youth.

"How do you want to go about this Cathy?" her grandmother was now by her side.

"I have been preparing, and feel I need to place myself apart from you all and try to call them to me. Not too far from you all though" Cathy replied.

Walking to what they all thought would be the centre of the main hall, Cathy touched her new bracelet and necklace, for confidence and protection.

"I call out to you Betty and John Holroyd, from the 1880s, you lived at Riverside Mills. Are you here?"

Cathy listened carefully, nothing. "Master of the Workhouse, Mr John Wood, are you here, to help me with my quest. Please show yourself if you are here."

Again, she heard nothing and felt nothing. "Mr and Mrs Holroyd, your daughter Clara Jane has contacted me. She did not run away; she was murdered in the mill. She was near you all the time. Please show yourself if you are still here and have not passed over."

Cathy waited, the others watched on, from a distance. Nothing, so she walked back over to the group. "Was there a church or a place where they might have done bible class?" She asked Gilbert, rather than the others.

"Here," he said, "look here, this small outbuilding is labelled Sunday Service Room. That could be what you are looking for.

Let's try and work out where this is on the maps. It looks to be on the other side of the apartment, near the back field.

They all trudged through the fields and let Cathy go ahead to see if she felt anything.

She used the same questions as before, concentrating so hard, she was nearly knocked over by a rush of chilled air.

"Who is there?" she asked the air rushing around her. "Please, one at once. Mr John Wood, are you here, please make yourself visible."

Cathy could hear a distant mumbling but could not make out any words. She did feel like there were a lot more than one ghost there.

"Mr Wood, Mr, and Mrs Holroyd. Please can you show yourself to me, I am Catherine Collins, the new ghost whisperer. Granddaughter of Sally Buckley, the deceased head of the Green Valley Coven. Clara Jane Holroyd has contacted me, she wishes to be reunited with her parents."

Cathy waited patiently, twiddling her bracelet as she waited. She gave a small thumbs up to the waiting group, just to let them know, so far, she was all right.

"Please show yourself, I want to grant Clara Jane her wishes, the poor child was pushed down the newly constructed lift shaft and has spent all these years alone. She would like to be reunited."

Slowly Cathy could feel the chill break away from her. In front of her she could begin to make out the outline of quite a sturdy gentleman.

"Are you Mr Wood, the Master of the Green Valley Workhouse, from the 1880s?" she nervously asked him. She still was not that used to seeing new ghosts.

"Aye, that be, I am him," the vision replied to her. "What is it you are wanting here, disturbing the poor people that got confined to this miserable place, me included."

"I am here to try to find John and Betty Holroyd. Betty died here in 1884 and John in 1885. They died believing their eldest daughter had run off with a wrong un from the Riverside mill back in 1883. She did not run away; she was pushed down a deep shaft and left to die alone."

"We have so many ghosts around here, how I will know who they are, if I ask, they will all claim to be her parents." Mr Wood told her, and Cathy understood his predicament, she hadn't thought of that.

"I will ask a question about Clara Jane; the correct parents will be the only one to know this." Cathy remembered about the first daughter called Clara Jane that died as an infant.

"Is there anything else I can help you with?" Cathy asked, as she felt that Mr Wood wasn't going to be much help at all.

"We have a number of ghosts at the old workhouse, some have waited a long time for their relatives. They now feel stuck, as they don't know how to pass over. Would you be able to help with that?" He replied, warming to her visit, as he felt she could help more than just him.

"Let me ask my colleagues" Cathy motioned the others to join her, reassuring Mr Wood that all was ok. "How can we help these people pass to the other side? They have been stranded here for many years, waiting for loved ones, how would we do it?"

Sally came forward first, and Mr Wood could see she was also a ghost. "How are you able to look human, yet you're a ghost?"

Sally smiled and went to him, "I am Sally Buckley, the leader of the Green Valley Circle of Dove Coven. I passed last year, but like you I chose to stay, in spirit form, until I reached out to my granddaughter. She has the power of the ghost whisperer, she will be able to help you and your friends to move on, if you let her help. First, we need to reunite Clara Jane with her parents John and Betty Holroyd. We have researched and found that they both died in the workhouse, shortly after Clara Jane allegedly ran away. She wants to make peace with them, herself. She was only fourteen when she was murdered."

Sally certainly had a way with the gentlemen folk. One could see Mr Wood quite taken with her.

"I will ask them to join us, but how will you know it is them?" Mr Wood asked Sally, forgetting everyone else present. "Cathy has a question for them, only the correct couple will pass the correct answer," she told him.

"Shall we try to bring them forward, please. You can tell the others, that I will research how we can help you all pass over to your peace." Cathy gently asked him. "Mr Wood, do you mind

117

me asking, when I researched the workhouse, I found out that your wife Emma also died young, have you been waiting for her?"

If ghosts could cry, this would have been the time. Mr Wood, the old Master of Green Valley Workhouse, practically broke down at the mention of his long-gone late wife. "Yes," he muttered, "I have waited so long, but she must have passed over straight away."

For a few moments everyone stood in their own thoughts. Every member of the party gathered on the top of the remote hill, had lost a loved one.

"Can you wait here?" he said, "I will be back soon, once I get the old folk to calm down. Young lady, you have caused quite a stir coming here today." He smiled as he disappeared from the earthly sight.

Cathy looked at the people she classed as friends, and they all smiled, encouraging her that it was going well. "What is the question you have for the parents?" Cynthia asked quietly.

"You will see soon, I hope. It isn't a trick question, but a personal one to John and Betty Holroyd, your own ancestors. Are you ready to meet them Cynthia?" Cathy held her arm, as she spoke to her.

"I have never had much family, now I have Clara Jane and may meet my own great grandparents. This is all because of you Cathy. Without your presence at the mill, through Sally, none of this would be possible, I don't know how to thank you." Cynthia was on the verge of tears.

Before Cathy could reply, Mr Wood's ghost reappeared, with him were three couples. All dressed in 1880s clothing.

"These three couples all say they are called Holroyd. Which I know they are, but can you ask them their Christian names Cathy, I think it be best that you do the talking." Mr Wood looked a little flustered, guessing that this was new to him too.

"Hi, my name is Cathy Collins, the new ghost whisper of Green Valley. I am here on a quest to reunite one of your families daughters with you. I have to be certain I have the correct parents. So could you all tell me your names, individually. Please do not worry, if you are not the correct set of parents, we are looking at all of you being able to pass over peacefully, to be reunited." Cathy saw one woman, take a deep intake of breath when she had mentioned the reunion.

The first couple introduced themselves as John and Sarah Holroyd. The second couple named themselves as John and Betty Holroyd, as did the third couple.

"Oh, this is a bit confusing," Cathy said. "I am sorry, but the first couple is not the correct family. Our child is from the parents of John and Betty,

"Can I ask, the two couples, what was the name of your child that you lost in 1883?" Cathy continued.

The couple that Cathy thought were the right couple, said their daughter Clara Jane ran off with a neighbour. But the second couple also claimed the same story.

Everyone felt a little uncomfortable, as it was now quite obvious that one of the couples were lying.

"Ok, couple number three, what was the name of the child that you lost, first of all, and when?" Cathy noticed there was a look of confusion on the couples face. "It was our Clara Jane, like we said in 1883, she ran off with that lad."

"Can I ask you two, the same question," she noticed that the woman was gently weeping, and her husband held her close. "We lost a baby girl in 1868, she died at a few days old." John Holroyd told the gathering.

Cathy walked to the couple and quietly said, "the baby had the same name didn't she, and died at a few days after birth." "Yes," John replied. "What did you mean Clara Jane was murdered, we were told she went off with that good for nothing lad?"

"I will tell you all about it, but for now we need some privacy with you. Mr Wood, could you take these other people back, and then return for John and Betty in a few minutes." Cathy was quite stern with her request, she did understand that the other couple were desperate to pass over, but it was not nice trying to claim Clara Jane as theirs.

"I will be back shortly and thank you Cathy. I think your visit today will lift a lot of peoples hopes now." He told the others to follow him, and left Cathy with John and Betty Holroyd, with Betty in tears.

119

"Right, I guess I better start from the beginning of what happened on that Sunday afternoon" Cathy began the story of Clara Jane and Marty sneaking into the mill after Sunday school. She told them of the push that ended their daughters life, she skipped a bit about her not passing right away. She needed to spare that detail for now. She brought them up to date and told her about how her spirit had been found and that she was now quite a happy young ghost of a girl. She introduced Cynthia as their great Granddaughter, their youngest son's descendant.

There were a lot of tears, but Cathy felt they were tears of relief and contentment.

"When can we meet Clara Jane," Betty spoke for the first time. "Can we all pass over together?"

"Yes, that is the plan, her remains have been located and are at the office of the coroner, as it was an historical murder. But once it is cleared, we will bury her remains in your grave plot. Then you will be together again"

Cathy turned to her grandmother, and their eyes passed a conversation that no one else saw. When should they get Clara Jane there to meet her parents, or do we take them to the mill?

"Let me go fetch her, these people can't wait any longer" Sally replied, "Don't forget to get her to change," reminded Cathy.

Sally disappeared and Cathy told John and Betty that Clara Jane was coming right away to see them. She had practiced leaving the mill. She also warned them, that she had become quite a 21st century girl too, by being in the mill with everyone.

Mr Wood returned to the group and asked where Sally had gone. Harold told him what had been happening, and that Clara Jane would be along soon to meet up with her beloved parents.

Again, Cathy thought she saw tears in his eyes. It wasn't long before Sally arrived back, with her very clean looking 1883 Clara Jane, all dressed in her Sunday best.

She ran directly to her mother and father, as everyone watched on, wiping their own tears of emotions away. How do you reunite a young child murdered in 1883 with her parents. Well Cathy had just done that.

After what seemed like hours, Cathy told everyone gathered that it was time to stop for the day for now. Clara Jane went back to the mill with Sally, and her parents went back, wherever it was, with Mr Wood.

"We will be back soon," Cathy told them, "I will work on the way to help you all pass over together,"

The drive back to the mill was quiet, everyone was in their own world and thoughts. What had actually just happened. No one could put it in words. On arriving at the mill car park, Sally and Clara Jane were waiting for them. The assembled group went into the board room, while Kim and Wendy brought coffee and sandwiches in.

"Well, that was an adventure." Betty summed up the visit, "I never in my old life thought I would see this day. How are you Cynthia, and you Clara Jane?"

"How do we help all the other ghosts to pass over?" Cathy asked, worried that she had promised more than she could do.

"Oh, that's easy," Betty replied," It is the same kind of spell for the banishment we did before. With you around Cathy, anything is possible, I dare say. We just have to change a few words and they will easily pass to the other side, if they are ready to do so."

Desdemona joined in, "Yes Cathy, the passing over spell is quite simple, we would need the candles and equipment we used before but use a different phrase or two. Once we get Clara Jane's funeral over with, we can send the others over in peace too. What a marvellous day, Sally your girl is incredible."

After coffee sandwiches and cake, Cathy made her excuses to go back to her apartment. This magic was wonderful, but it took its toll. Clara Jane joined her on the walk back through the maze of corridors to the apartment. They left the older generation to catch up with the rest of the Coven, that had now also appeared.

Back at the apartment, Cathy saw that Clara Jane was looking sad, "What's the matter?" she asked the young ghost.

"When you talk about my funeral, it upsets me. I have been dead so long, and now I am getting some sort of life, even if I am a ghost. I do not want to be buried. I want to stay here with you and Sally and Cynthia. Is it wrong to want to stay. I can visit my parents grave once I know where it is. But I am not ready to leave the mill and disappear off this world yet. Please Cathy, please say I can stay here." Clara Jane was in floods of tears, and

Cathy had no idea what to say or do, she could not hug her. She needed her Gran now.

As if by magic, well it was magic, Sally appeared in the lounge with the two of them. "Have I missed something?" she said looking concerned firstly at Cathy and then Clara Jane.

Clara Jane flew across the room to Sally and held on to her so tight, and told her how she didn't want to leave, and have a funeral. How she was scared of leaving everyone to go somewhere she didn't know. That she wanted to be with Sally, Pearl, and Ruby, and all the ghosts in the mill together.

"Come here my child, "Sally comforted the weeping child ghost. "no one is making you go away. The remains of your earthly body will be buried in the grave with your parents, and you will be able visit there and talk to them whenever you like. There will always be a place here for you, with us at the mill. As long as you want to be here."

Cathy breathed a heavy sigh of relief, "Oh Gran, thank goodness you are here with me, I have no idea how all this works".

"We will have to tell the Coven, and maybe the magical police" Sally winked at Cathy with the mention of the MPA and Adam. "The funeral will take place once the remains are released. Clara Jane's parents can pass over with the others from the workhouse, it can be done all at the same time, I am sure".

Clara looked so happy, she as playing with her citrine bracelet and smiled shyly at Cathy. "My bracelet is my lucky charm, and Pearl and Ruby have asked if I can make them both one, would that be possible Cathy?"

A quick change of subject was good for them all, and they all went into the shop to sort out some stones for the new ghost bracelets. If only Clara Jane could make ones for retails sale smiled Cathy,

Chapter 23

Shapeshifters, Dinner, and Uncle Charles's

After a few days of visiting the workhouse and running her online shop; the weekend arrived for Cathy's evening date with Adam. She was looking forward to visiting his place, she didn't really know where he lived, even though they had met on numerous occasions now and he had been to her apartment at the mill occasionally.

Clara Jane helped her pick out her outfit, not too sexy, but at the same time a smart, bodycon black dress, medium height heels and a small amount of makeup. Cathy felt nervous at being invited to his house, but at the same time, she felt feminine again, a feeling her ex had more or less knocked out of her.

Right on time, she heard his car horn, in the car park in front of the shop. She used this entrance more and more, as she knew her ex wouldn't set foot near there in case Alf or Eric were around.

Cathy said night to Clara Jane. Who was off to spend the evening with Pearl and Ruby, they were more than happy with their new bracelets, and had taken Clara Jane back under their wings.

Cathy went through the shop and made sure to lock the door and shutter behind her, she climbed into Adams car, and received a kiss on her cheek. "*How romantic*" she thought to herself.

"Evening Cathy, you look amazing," Adam complimented. "I hope you have room for some food, I have been busy all day," he laughed, as they both knew that magic would be involved.

He did not have to drive far, as it seemed he actually lived on the edge of the land, belonging to the mill itself. There was a small complex of four large, detached house, within a gated compound.

"It looks very secure her," Cathy noted. "I didn't realise you were only round the corner," she laughed.

"Like you I have the small cottage in town, and this was the family home, until mum passed on. Dad actually lives in one of the larger houses in the mill drive, and as you know Gramps lives on the top floor of the mill, near Dessi".

"What's with the gates?" Cathy asked, "Are they there for any reason?" She sensed she knew the answer before it left her lips.

"Yes, Dave and Nigel, the archaeologist brothers live in the first one, Peter and Susie live in the second one. The third house were Roger, the solicitor lives, and I have the one on the end, over there. The reason for the gates, apart from security, is the fact that we are all shapeshifters of some sort. I know you have met Alf and Eric; they are shape shifting giants. They live with their wives, Rimmon and Rowan up on the hilltop, in a large house, that is built into the hillside, an amazing place. I will show you one day. Dave and Nigel are werewolves. So, the gates try to keep them out of trouble on full moons. Peter and Susie, and Roger are like me, witches, and wizards, with the ability to shapeshift. I hope you can to, it is amazing to fly out at night, I like to switch to an owl or eagle at times."

"Wow, that is a lot of information you have just given me, how do you learn to change shape," Cathy replied, her heart beating six to a dozen.

"Sorry, I blurted it all out, I did not know how to approach the subject. So, I just said it, are you ok with it all," Adam looked so nervous.

"Oh yes, of course, this new magical life just keeps getting better and better. I will ask Sally tomorrow if I can change, she will make me wait till after Clara Janes funeral no doubt. Did I tell you Clara Jane wants to stay with us at the mill, and not pass over with her parents. She wants a chance at some sort of living now. I cannot say I blame her."

"Dad told me, that Harold had let him know. He said you were brilliant at the old workhouse and that no one would get one pass you. Dad also told me that I had to tell you about the shape shifting and everything. I have to keep nothing from you. Are you really ok with all this?" Adam seemed nervous, he liked Cathy a lot, and didn't want any secrets, which was what his first wife had accused him of in the past.

"Absolutely, I am learning new things every day, maybe we can have dinner with the others one day, well if your food is up to scratch, did I tell you I am starving?" Cathy laughed so sweetly and kissed Adam on his cheek.

The electronic gates opened for them, and Adam drive his car to the driveway of the house at the end of the cul-de-sac. He got out and helped Cathy out of the car. He led her to the front door and let them inside. The smell of dinner greeted them as they walked in.

"Make yourself at home, kick your shoes off if you want, let's go through to the kitchen. I think that's a great idea to have a celebration dinner when the excavation and funeral is all completed. Now what would you like to drink?" Adam led her through into one of the grandest, biggest kitchens she had ever seen.

"Wow, this is an incredible kitchen, are you sure it is just you that are living here?" Cathy looked around her, the kitchen had a conservatory extension and lots of small white and golden lights flickered all along the roof.

"Yes, it is just me, I had to buy the wife out of it, when she left for better things, more money, all she ever wanted was money," a hint of irony came over his voice. "Yes, just like your ex."

"Well, we are both without them now, and it is for us two to enjoy this evening and all this food smells so good. Let's get started, a nice white wine for me," and she reached up to kiss him again, but made for his lips this time, and got the response for which she had hoped.

The evening passed in the same style, kisses, food, wine. The evening rolled on, when suddenly Adam became serious. "I forgot to tell you; I researched your Uncle Charles. It seems he was in the normal police, quite high up too. It went against his principles to be associated with witchcraft and had your Aunt and Elizabeth's magic bound by an old wizard, that made a real mess of doing it.

Audrey was so besotted with Charles and his position in society, and his family money; that she gave up her own family for him. Sally, herself will fill I on more details, I am sure."

Elizabeth is a younger version of her father, anything for money and lifestyle. We are sure, she knows nothing of her own family witchcraft. She was sent away to an expensive boarding school, where she mixed with mega rich families. All she ever wanted was more money. Apparently, she is telling everyone that your ex is a wealthy man too. She doesn't seem to have had a relationship before, no one was good enough for her or her father.

Charles inherited from his own paternal uncle, and that is the house they live in now. Elizabeth has her own annex, like I thought, but it is in reality, the converted garage. The money he got from work was never enough for him, it is rumoured that some of his work was not on the most legal side of things, and that he had a stash of ill gained money in his safe. It was never proved, as the people in his police force didn't really like him, he was always pompous and better than the rest. When he took early retirement, his party was more out of relief of him leaving. Sad really, is not it. What a waste of a magical lifestyle."

Cathy listened, intently "I wonder how much she knew my mother, or what it was like growing up with a sister? She must have been older than my mum, although I don't remember her or my dad very well."

"Let's change the subject from your aunt and uncle, and both our exes. Would madam like some pudding and some more wine?"

"Definitely," Cathy followed Adam into the luxurious kitchen again, they had had their meal in the dining room, which was in the conservatory. "Yummy my favourite, you must be a mind reader," she laughed as he pulled a huge pavlova from the walk-in fridge.

"Oh no," she blushed," you're not a mind reader too, oh no!"

"What on earth have you been thinking about to make you blush like that?" he teased her, grabbing her hand and pulling her in for yet another smoochy kiss.

(I think the rest of the evening should be left to the two grown up adults.)

Chapter 24

Clara Jane's Funeral

The day had finally arrived for the remains of Clara Jane's body to be placed in the grave with her parents. Many a conversation had been held, with all the parties involved. Clara Jane was going to stay at the mill, under the watchful eye of Cynthia, Sally, Pearl, Ruby, and Cathy.

Her parents were ready to pass over, to re-join their baby daughter and sons, and their grandchildren that had already passed on. There were also another fifteen ghosts from the workhouse wanting to pass over to. They had for too long been waiting for their loved ones and hoped they would find them on the other side. Mr Wood, the old master said a few were staying behind, but would Cathy call and see them occasionally to see if they were ready. She had agreed but said they could always find her at the mill, or Sally.

Clara Jane was bouncing around the place; she was ecstatic that she was allowed to stay as a ghost and to learn about the things in the shop. She wanted to wear jeans and modern clothes, to watch her own burial, and to say goodbye to her parents, for now. But Sally had talked her around, and she was now wearing a modern-day version of her old smock, with knee length boots, her hair pinned back, and face scrubbed. She looked nothing like the poor young girl that they had found crying on the top floor all those months ago.

Everyone had agreed to meet at the old churchyard, where the gravediggers had reopened the large old tombstone from her parents grave. A procession of cars followed the hearse through the lanes to the churchyard. All the people that had come into contact with Clara Jane were out today. Clara Jane, Sally, and the other ghosts floated alongside the hearse to the graveyard.

Cathy, Adam, Harold, and Cynthia were in the lead car, following the tiny coffin in the front car. They had chosen a small white coffin to place all her remains in. The coroner and undertaker had taken great care with the remains and tried their best to lay them out in the proper form of a skeleton. Her small leather shoes and the penny were placed in the coffin with her. Clara Jane had made a small bracelet that she asked to go with her remains, for protection.

As they approached the old churchyard, Cathy felt the cold shift of the older ghosts waiting for them.

They parked the car, behind the hearse. Alf and Eric carried the small coffin between them, past the other old graves to the freshly opened one at the far end of the church yard. Even the vicar of the church had come along to the burial. It wasn't everyday occurrence that a young girl missing for 140 years got to be laid to rest with her parents.

Cathy and Adam followed the coffin, to the final resting place. Cathy saw Sally with her arm around poor Clara Jane. Just behind them, Cathy saw the ghosts of John and Betty Holroyd, the mother was still crying, but John held her tight to him.

The vicar said a few words and the coffin was lowered into the ground. The gathered people threw a few flowers on the coffin and the gravediggers swiftly pulled a green carpet over the open tomb.

It had been decided that after the burial, the ghosts of the workhouse, with Cathy and her friends, would go to the site of the old workhouse Sunday school. Desdemona and Betty had brought the equipment to help send the weary ghosts over to the other side.

It was sad to see such a small coffin go down into the cold dark grave, but seeing Clara Jane floating along with her parents, Cathy felt she had completed the quest set to her by Cynthia, when they first met. So much she had learnt since then, and a lot more to learn too. Top of the list was shape-shifting so she could go flying with Adam and his friends over the valley.

Eventually the small crowd gathered at the old site of the Green Valley workhouse. Cathy and Sally went over to Clara Jane and her parents. Time for them to say their goodbyes. Cathy's heart broke for Clara Jane, she had only been reunited for a short time. But she knew that letting her stay was the right thing to do.

Desdemona, Cynthia, Pat, and Betty, from the Coven, laid out the candles and the chalked hexagon shape. Cathy had her grimoire with her this time, she had learned the words by heart, but she felt more confidence holding the magic book.

Time to start. Harold and Gilbert stood together, they looked more like twins than cousins. Cathy was going to have to find out more about the two of them, they looked such characters.

Pearl and Ruby stood with Clara Jane, as her parents went to join the other ghosts ready to pass over to the other side. "Thank you, Cathy," Betty told her as she passed her to join the others. "To know that she is going to be looked after now, after all she suffered, is all that a mother can wish for. May you have the happiness you deserve my love."

Cathy joined the other witches in the hexagon, and the chanting started, A little louder than when banishing the bullies from the mill. This time it was respectful, Cathy let her mind concentrate on the task ahead of her. She felt the words rush through her body, the warmth of the magic. She felt she was being lifted off the ground. She saw each face as the ghost passed over into whichever spirit world it was that they believed in.

Mr Wood stopped and mouthed thank you to her. The final ones to pass were John and Betty Holroyd, Betty slowed to show Cathy the babe in her arms. They had been reunited at the graveside when Clara Jane's coffin had been lowered in. Two happy parents, one content baby and one contented young lady happy to stay behind them, to make up for her lost years.

Eventually Cathy collapsed in the waiting arms of Adam, she was spent, he lifted her and carried her gently back to the waiting car. Straight back to the mill apartment and for a long rest.

On their return to the mill, Sally and Clara Jane were waiting for them. Everyone else had gone to the board room for coffee and cakes, but Sally told Cathy to rest. The energy she had spent on that spell, would take a few days for her to recover.

Clara Jane was so excited, she came over to hug Cathy, and very nearly managed to touch her. "What was that?" Cathy asked her grandmother.

"Now that you are basically her legal ghostly guardian, she will one day be able to do most of the things I can do, and yes that means hug you, and help in the shop!" Sally smiled at her granddaughter.

"What you have done today, Cathy, is absolutely incredible. Adam, will you stay with her, and address her every need, as she deserves. Clara Jane and I are going to go and join in her wake!" and with that the two ghosts disappeared from the apartment.

"Can I get you anything, Cathy. You were amazing today in that field, I saw Betty Holroyd show you the tiny baby too. You made so many people or ghosts happy today. You are one wonderful woman." Adam knelt beside her on the sofa and realised that she was fast asleep. Grabbing a blanket from the bedroom, he curled up next to her and held her tight. He knew he was slowly falling in love with this amazing woman.

Chapter 25

The Cabin in the Woods

After the excitement of the last few days, Cathy and Adam decided to take a few days off work, and escape to the country. They had left strict instructions to only be contacted in an emergency. Although Cathy thought, everything with Clara Jane had been sorted now. She was spending her days with Cynthia, and her nights with Pearl and Ruby, exploring the mill and further afield, as ghosts do not sleep.

They set off, in Adams car. Cathy was nervous as it had been a good while since she had spent any time away with a man, on her own. Although she could magic her clothes, she had packed her newly bought lingerie. Kim and Wendy had taken her shopping the day before, specifically for some new clothes. She had blushed to start with, but when she tried on the black lacey outfit, she knew it was perfect for her.

"Where are we heading too," Cathy snuggled up to Adam as he drove away from Green Valley.

"Not too far away, I don't want to spend our break driving. I thought we could head towards the coast, I have booked a small log cabin, I thought we could do the cooking ourselves, with a little magic help." Adam smiled; he was feeling incredibly lucky spending time alone with this wonderful woman; who didn't quite know herself how amazing she was. He thought her ex was a man that didn't know good luck when it stared him in the fac., Then he thought of his ex, and felt she was just the same as Martin.

"What are you smiling at?" Cathy asked him.

"I was just thinking that your ex and mine, they would make a wonderful couple. I was thinking of how lucky I am to be spending time with you. Without them two being so stupid, we would never have met." Adam smiled at her, and Cathy's stomach flipped, she knew she had strong feelings for him, even so soon in their relationship, and she was getting the impression he was too.

"So, a secluded cottage in the woods, just the two of us. What on earth will we do with the spare time?" Cathy teased him.

"I am sure we will think of something, hot tub, outside fire pit, plenty of food and wine. Plenty of chatting and get to know each other." Adam slowed the car and looked at his passenger. "I hope you like it; it looked an amazing place on the internet."

"I am sure I will, it's a shame it is only a couple of days. So we better make the most of it."

After just under two hours, they drove down the long country lane to the small group of exclusive log cabins. Adam checked them in, and they drove and found their home for the next few days.

On opening the door to the wooden cabin, Cathy realised it was no ordinary log cabin. "Wow, I never knew this place existed, how did you find it?"

"It is part of the magical police agency secret locations. I have never been before, but I remember one of the detectives coming here, once after a real nasty case. He told me if I ever want to take someone somewhere special, it must be here. Magic is all around, and it is totally private."

Cathy explored the cabin, there was plush white furniture in the lounge, the bathroom had a jacuzzi, double walk shower and even a sauna. The bedroom was the finest she had ever seen, and it had patio doors that opened on the decking that surrounded the cabin. The hot tub looked very inviting, and around the next corner was the purpose-built fire pit. Which was actually an outdoor gas heater, dug into the ground. Recliners and hammocks dotted around the patio, twinkling lights finished off the wow factor.

The kitchen was filled already with their favourite food and drinks. Adam laughed, "the booking agent asked what kind of things we liked, I think they got it just right. Would madam like a drink and try the hot tub. I quite fancy the idea of sitting in the hot bubbling water, with the trees around us, and chillout time. What do you think?"

"Absolutely," Cathy was thinking of the new bikini she had bought, hoping for this occasion, "Sounds perfect to me. With it being late afternoon, let's hope for a fabulous sunset to watch." Cathy and Adam made themselves at home in the cabin. While Cathy got unpacked and ready to spend time in the hot tub, Adam lit the fire pit and prepared a very resplendent picnic for them to eat while relaxing.

As the sun was setting, the pair climbed into the warm bubbling water, and watched as the sky turned from light blue to midnight blue, with a hint of a red sunset. They counted the stars; they laughed and told each other their family history. Adam had known from a young age his abilities and had even attended a magical school. His mother had passed over a few years ago, leaving just him and his dad, Brian. Being an only child, he was close to his dad and grandfather. They had all worked together at one time. He recalled some amusing stories of life as a magical detective. The mischievous elves at Christmas, making life difficult for the community, he laughed and told Cathy that they slept most of the year, and came out for the Santa Season.

"What on earth is the Santa Season? Do you mean Christmas in general?" Cathy quizzed.

"It's when the enchanted mill comes to life, you must have wondered what is behind all the closed shutters and in the cellar of the mill?" Adam teased her.

"Are you telling me, that behind those shutters, are an army of elves, that help Father Christmas?", she laughed. "And what is in that cellar, that it is so out of bounds?"

"I certainly am, I know you have had to learn so much, so quick, but Christmas at the Mill is actually magical. But the cellar is strictly out of bounds!"

He held her close and clinked her glass. "I hope we get to spend Christmas together Cathy," he whispered in her ear, before kissing her passionately. She let the subject change to some more smooching, but knew it was one she would bring up again, soon.

The following couple of days the newly lovebirds spent their time, walking, talking, and kissing. Escaping from reality in the incredible environment. All too soon it was time to return to the real, albeit magical world.

"I suppose we had better turn our phones back on," said Cathy reluctantly. She had had the most wonderful time at the enchanted cabin in the woods, with Adam.

As they drove away from their magical holiday cabin, Cathy switched on both of their phones, as soon as they got a signal, both phones beeped with text message coming through.

"So much for not being in contact with us," she laughed. "I will read mine, while you drive."

"Hope it isn't too bad," Adam commented, as he heard the beeps coming through on Cathy's phone. "It's odd" Cathy said a bit confused. The first ones are from Uncle Charles. We have been unobtainable for just over 48 hours, and there are ten messages and missed calls. Here is a voice mail from Harold at the mill, lets listen.

"Cathy and Adam, Harold here. We all hope you have had a good break from Green Valley. Just wanted to let you know that your aunt and uncle have been to see me at the mill, chasing up on you. When you do get this message, could you give me a ring back and I can update you. Thank you."

"Well, that sounds ominous," Adam said. "Sounds like something to do with Elizabeth and her fiancée. If I think about it, it has been quiet for a while. What do you feel about it Cathy?"

"I had better ring him, at least they did not phone the reception and spoil our break. So, it can't be that much of an emergency."

"I will ring Harold first. I am not keen on speaking to someone who is supposed to be my uncle to be honest." She replied to Adam, whilst dialling Harold's direct line.

The phone didn't ring long, before Harold answered. He must have known it was Cathy, as he answered straight away. "Well, hello you two, how have you been. I assume you have got my message. Your Aunt and Uncle have visited your shop unit, a couple of times. On the last occasion, I had Alf to bring them around to the board room. They actually want your advice! How that woman is Sally's daughter, I have no idea. Seems they are having a problem with their daughters fiancé."

"Well, we have had a wonderful, few days. Thank you for asking. Sounds odd that they have come to see me. I wonder if he has let slip that we have history together, what shall I do?" Cathy asked Harold, as Adam listened to the conversation.

"I am sure it can wait until we get back," Adam said, as Cathy had put the phone on loudspeaker.

"Yes of course," Harold told them, "They would not tell me much, and of course they cannot see Sally, as she is a ghost. When you get back and unpack, could we all meet in the boardroom, with Roger to discuss the next steps?"

"Can we make it tomorrow morning," Adam suggested. "We were stopping off for lunch on our way home. I am sure a few more hours will keep."

"Of course, shall we say 10.00am at the solicitors office. So, we can help to prepare Cathy for her meeting with Charles and Audrey?" answered Harold. "I am sorry for breaking this to you on your return, I didn't expect you to switch your phone on as soon as you left."

He laughed to himself, reminiscing about young couples being in love. He had been there himself, back in the day, but he went away to war, and when he had eventually got back to Green Valley, Sally had married Walter. He had been listed as missing, presumed dead. Yet he had been in a prisoner of war camp, and then rehabilitation. He had got back to Green Valley, four years too late. He did not resent them marrying, but he still adored that woman. Now, he smiled, in one respect he had got her by his side again.

"Ok, that sounds great, we will see you at Rogers at 10.00 am, and thank you for warning us," Cathy concluded the phone call.

"Well. I wonder what that means, have they got married without telling them, run away or even both," Cathy laughed," now tell me about this lunch stop?"

Chapter 26
The Ex and his New Wife Disappear

Cathy and Adam collected Harold from the mill, at 9.30am the following morning, and drove across town to the solicitors office. Roger was waiting in the reception and led them through to his office.

"Morning everyone, Cathy you look radiant, the break most have done you good. Fabulous work for Clara Jane and the workhouse crowd, you really are proving to be Sally's ancestor. Speaking of Sally's descendants, Audrey and Charles have been to see you, and I believe left you lots of messages about Elizabeth. We are under the impression that they have learnt some of his history. We need to find out what they know, and why they are chasing you. If they know about Martin, they are not going to be happy, but if he and Elizabeth have run off, we need them on our side. To help save their inheritance from him. He may have found out the worth of his future in laws, that might be why they have contacted you, as a relative."

"Shall I ring him back, and ask how I can help them? Play innocent for now?" Cathy suggested.

"Yes, while we are all here, and can listen in. He was not known to be the brightest person in the force, so let us get out of him what he knows." Roger replied.

"Ok, then let's get this done, and out of the way." Cathy nervously rang the number in her phone and let it ring.

"Hello, who is this?" the gruff voice answered.

"Hi, it is Catherine, your niece, you left me some messages on my mobile. But I have been on holiday and there was no phone signal, so I am returning your call," she said sweetly through gritted teeth.

"Ha yes, good," he replied, "We wondered if we could meet up with you, that is your Aunt and myself. We would like to ask you a couple of questions, if you didn't mind."

"Of course, that would be great to meet up. What sort of questions would you like to ask me?" Cathy tried to get him to tell her.

"Bit awkward really, I am not used to this sort of thing. But your Aunt and I would like some help from you, regarding Elizabeth and this fella of hers. We have reason to believe, that you might know him, and were he could be. As you see, we had a falling out about him and she went off with him. In our opinion he seems to be just after her money – and ours." Cathy almost felt sorry for him.

Roger passed her a written note, asking her to invite them to the solicitors office – as soon as they could. They now needed to be told the full extent of their future son in law.

"I am actually with my solicitor in town, and we wondered if you would like to come over. There are a few questions we are already going through about them. If you could come over, I will explain all to you. Would that be, ok?" Cathy asked, trying not to give too much away, and got the thumbs up from Adam.

"You are at Rogers place?" he asked, "we can be over in twenty minutes, being a retired policeman, I sniff something isn't right – is that the case?"

"I am afraid so, Uncle Charles, please get over as soon as feasible, and we will fill you in. Another police brain will help us mightily." Smiling at the creeping on her behalf, she ended the call.

"Well, Cathy that went better than expected, he has smelt a rat, and time we came clean; and help save his money too. If we can cut off the inheritance before she tries to claim it, at least that will help some way," Roger said.

"Let's have coffee and cake whilst we wait," Roger suggested, and everyone took a deep breath as they waited for the arrival of Aunt Audrey and Uncle Charles. They didn't have long to wait, and Cathy was horrified at the state her Aunt was in.

"What in earth as happened," she asked her, leading her to a chair and getting a coffee for her.

"Oh Catherine, I am so sorry, we haven't been good relations. Martin told us that you were his first wife, and that you let him down with no inheritance and that he was going to take us to the cleaners. All because we disagreed with them getting married so quickly." She said through her tears.

"You mean they have already got married?" Cathy said, aghast," Oh no, we had hoped to stop that."

"What do you mean? Why didn't you tell us before?" Charles shouted.

"Calm down Charles," Harold snapped, let me explain.

"Yes, Catherine was married to the scoundrel a few years ago, he abused her and demanded money of her and her Uncle John. He left her and married within weeks of their divorce. The MPA are involved as we feel he has been married a few times and isn't yet divorced. We asked Catherine not to say anything, to lull him into a false security. Then we were going to pounce on him and put him away for a long time. Did you know he went to the mill a few weeks ago, broke into Catherine's unit, assaulted her, and stole money? No, we did not think so. You have not been kind to Catherine after all the troubles she has had in her short life. So we let Elizabeth croon about her new love, in the hope we could find his last wife, and stop the romance. Seems like we were too late."

"What, oh, oh dear, "Audrey sobbed.

"Where are they now, when did they marry, and under what name," Adam gently asked the distraught couple.

"We do not know where they are now, they came round to our house two days ago, and showed us the marriage certificate and the matching rings. That fella had such a superior look on his face, as we had told them to wait before marrying." Charles now seemed to be letting the words roll out, as if unburdening.

"They came round last week, and being the actor he is, he actually asked my permission to marry my daughter. We said we were all for it, we felt pleased Elizabeth had met someone at last, but we asked them to wait before they married, to make sure they were compatible. Then he started shouting and ranting, Elizabeth was in tears. That's when he said that you had been talking. We were so confused, as we had no idea you knew him. He told us that you were married to him and that you were a useless wife, with no inheritance at all, and that Elizabeth was now his."

Audrey was sobbing in her chair and Cathy put her arm around her. "It will be alright, but he is only after the money, when we find him, he will be in prison for a long time. When he was at the mill, in his old car, one of the security guards put a tracker on the car, we can find out where the car is, that should give us a lead. Did you let Elizabeth have all the money from her grandmother's house sale? Does she have any more money in her name? I don't like asking personal questions, but he is only out for the money. We are trying to track down his last wife, but she was last seen on a cruise ship, and no one has seen her since."

Charles stood up and walked in circles around the office. "When the house sale went through so smoothly, we were a bit shocked, I did tell her to put the money away in a 30-day bond, so she couldn't spend it all at once. She doesn't have much of her own money, as she has never worked and lives rent free in her own flat, next to the house. She has an allowance from my parents estate that she lives off. The money from the house sale went to her head and she spent a small fortune on clothes and a car – that is still in the garage at home. I physically made her go to the bank, and she did put £150,000 into different ISAs and savings accounts. Can we put a stop on that money?"

Roger spoke first. "We can ask the bank if it is possible under the circumstances, as it is a legal matter. But she still as the remains of £50,000 to spend?"

"I can do that", Adam said. "We have a special relationship with the bank in these sorts of matters. We don't want him getting his hands on anything else. Is Elizabeth the sole inheritor for your property too?"

"Yes, she is, can I do anything about that?" he asked the solicitor.

"Yes, we can add an addendum to the will, that she must not be with this person. What name was on the marriage certificate, can you remember, He has been called Bradshaw, Bradbury, Bradgate to name a few.?"

"It was Bradgate, I remember the certificate, as I am sure he once called himself Bradbury, but it all happened so fast." Audrey answered. "After the awful behaviour, he grabbed Elizabeth's arm and left the house. We didn't see them for a few days, and she didn't answer her phone. When they turned up two days ago, they had been to Gretna Green, and they had got married there. She looked so happy to have a ring on her finger.

Bless the poor child, we have kept her so close all these years. She deserves some happiness, but sadly not like this."

"Can I ask, why you say she has been kept so close, what do you mean," Cathy acted all innocently, knowing full well her uncles actions.

"It is a long story Catherine," Charles started, "I appreciate I am in a room with magical people, and I admit it has taken me a lot to ask your help. When I first met Audrey, I knew her mother was the head of the Green Valley Coven. In my position in the police, I didn't want any magic in my family. Audrey and I were in love, and I hoped she accepted my behaviour back then. I asked a local wizard to bind her own powers, and then the same for Elizabeth. I was too proud back then to be involved in magic. I have regretted the decision over the years, as I know Audrey missed her mother, and her younger sister. But the past can't be undone, can it? But please, I ask, can you help us find Elizabeth and put this fella in prison for good?"

Everyone went quiet, no one had expected his full confession so quickly. They sat and watched as Charles sobbed as he held Audrey close. He had been protecting his small family, never knowing that magic could have helped them. She had lost her mother and her sister, to please him.

"Yes, yes, we will do all we can to find your daughter, and if you like, we can help rectify the magic position if you ever find you want to." Harold joined in the conversation.

"I messaged Alf, our security man, and the tracker says the old Celica is down in Southampton, my guess would be that they are on a cruise again,"

"Another cruise, what is it with this man?" Cathy muttered, "I guess we can call the docks for the boat the car is registered too."

"I don't know how to thank you for helping us," Charles began, "Audrey, would you like your powers unbound. The example that Catherine is setting with her magical powers is just incredible. Yes, we have heard about the excavation at the mill, most of Green Valley as, magical, and non-magical community. The work with the old workhouse occupants has spread though all communities Catherine. Well done girl."

Audrey looked dumbfounded, she never expected to hear her husband of so many years, offer to let her practice her magic again. "Can we find Elizabeth first please."

"We cannot alert Elizabeth to the legal case being built against her now husband, we should let her enjoy a few weeks as a new bride," Cathy told the group. "Let us hope we have everything in place for when they disembark and then we arrest him then. When we have everything in place. We need to find the cruise they are on, get copies of all the marriage certificates, try to find wife number two, and make a file on the assault and break-in at my unit."

"You are so like your mother," Audrey told her, "Full of empathy and so organised. Thank you, Catherine."

So, it was agreed to get all the details together, copy certificates, put a stop on the bank accounts, find the bank records with various names, collect relevant CCTV and the elusive second wife.

After more coffee and cake, the group dispersed, everyone found their own niche job and Adam took Cathy and Harold back to the mill.

Walking back through the maze of corridors, Adam and Cathy laughed, as their trip away, was now just a memory, back down to earth with a bump.

Chapter 27

The Crystal Seller

As usual, life soon got back to normal. Cathy and Adam became even closer. Her own cottage in the village, was more or less empty now and she wondered what to do with it. For now, she was ok, maybe in a few months she could get a tenant for it.

She was busy sorting out her orders, a few days after the meeting with her Aunt and Uncle. Sally had been interested in the meeting and Charles actually more or less admitted regretting his part in Audrey's magical binding. She laughed that Elizabeth was just as impulsive as her mother, she too had warned Audrey about marrying the pompous Charles, but she still went ahead and married him. She also added it would be nice if they could reconcile too.

Clara Jane was singing to herself, some pop tune she had seen on the TV. Her jewellery making was coming on fast and now her skills meant that Cathy had more jewellery to sell online, she didn't advertise that it was made by a ghost, but it was called the Spirit Collection,

Cathy checked her email and found an email from someone she didn't recognise. When she opened it, it turned out to be the crystal seller from the Festival in the Field. As she read the email, she felt a cold shiver go down her back and goosebumps in her arms.

"Hi, I was wondering if you were interested in buying my stock, I have followed your online shop, and didn't know who else to turn to. I run my small business from my house in Upper Valley and attend various festivals. Recently my husband left me, and cleared out the bank account, I wondered if you would be interested in buying my stock, as I have to find money to keep a roof over my head. Kind regards, Gillian Bradshaw"

"Oh no, it can't be, can it," Cathy shouted to Clara Jane, Sally, and Oskar. "Come look at this email I have just received."

"It could well be," Sally put her arm on her, "Fate moves in mysterious ways does not it. But if this is the second wife, then it is the final piece in the evidence. Arrange to meet her for coffee and I will stay in the background to listen in." Detective Sally said. "You had better tell Adam, and I will go and inform Harold."

Cathy rang Adam and explained about the email. She knew he would say play it cautious to start with, as that is what she would do. Show interest in the stock and delay a day or two. Find out a much as possible about the ex and play sympathy. She felt he was reading her mind again.

Cathy replied to the email:

"Hi Gillian, thank you for your email, I am sorry to read about your unfortunate circumstances. Yes, I would be interested in your stock, I saw your stall at the Festival in the Field, a couple of months ago. Would you like to meet up for coffee and cake and have a chat. Regards Cathy

Part of Cathy felt sympathy for this woman, she knew little about her, if it was the second wife; but the odds seem perfect to say it was.

A few emails later, and Cathy had arranged to meet Gillian later that day at the small café, just on the border of Green Valley and Upper Valley, well it was more of a garden centre than just a café.

She updated Adam, and he told her that Martin and Elizabeth had been tracked onto a 21-day cruise around the Mediterranean. So wouldn't be back for at least two weeks, leaving plenty of time to get all the evidence in order for when he stepped off the cruise ship. He said not to mention anything to Gillian, it might not be the second wife. But to keep on her amethyst ring, in case she needed Alf and Eric as back up.

That made Cathy felt a little nervous, she hadn't thought that there may be any danger involved.

She set off in her little car, down the country lanes to the planned meeting place. All she knew about the second wife was she was small and a red head, and thinking back, the woman on the stall at the festival had been small. She wondered if she had seen Martin at the field, but of course not if they were still married, he would have avoided her.

As soon as she walked into the café, and saw the redhead sat waiting for her, Cathy knew exactly who she was. She also knew, that the woman had no idea who Cathy was.

"Hi, is it Gillian?" Cathy said as she walked to the table by the window.

"Hi back, yes, I am Gillian, sorry I look such a mess, I have not slept for weeks. My husband is a strange man, he often disappears for weeks on end, but always comes back. This time, the money from the bank as all gone, and I just don't know what to do."

"Let's go and get a coffee and have a chat," Cathy's heart went out to this woman, she had been in this situation a few years ago, and it looked like the same man.

Cathy let Gillian do all the talking, poor woman had been used by this husband for years now. But she knew she had to ask the question, was it the same man?

"Tell me Gillian, when did you meet this man, what was his name again?" tactfully Cathy asked her.

"Martin, he is called Martin." She began, "I met him online about four years ago, I fell completely. It was uncanny, as my parents had both just died, and I had come into a bit of money. I thought, to myself, at last, I have someone to enjoy my time with. I had looked after my parents for years, and not really had a life. I loved my crystals even back then and I escaped to the festivals when I could. He didn't like the crystal business; pebbles he called them. Once we were married, we went on a three-week cruise around the Mediterranean, paid for by me. I might add now, looking back, I feel such a fool".

"I think we have more in common than just crystals Gillian. I would like to introduce you to a couple of my colleagues, if you don't mind, and then we can explain what we think is happening. Out of curiosity, how much did he steal from you?" Cathy could not help herself from asking.

"I don't understand what you mean, Cathy," Gillian looked confused," I came here to sell you the stock, and get enough money for the rent."

Cathy showed Gillian a photograph of Martin, "Is this your husband?"

144

"Yes, how have you got a photograph of my husband?" Gillian asked, she was getting a little fidgety.

"Because, he was my husband once, and we believe he has just remarried. Shall we go and meet my solicitor and the detective. I will update you in the way to the office. Please, you are safe with me, and I will help you with your rent, I promise" Cathy held onto Gillian's hand to reassure her everything would be ok.

Cautiously Gillian, looked at Cathy, "You were his wife? He never said he had another wife."

"We were married just out of university, and it did not last long. I did not inherit the money he expected. Please come and meet Adam and Roger, they will explain it all to you. We are looking for him, as he broke into my unit and assaulted me a few weeks ago, he thought I had come into some money."

"I don't know what it is, Cathy, but I trust you 100%, lead the way. I think I have just arrived at my senses after all this time."

Cathy rang Adam and he agreed to meet them at the solicitors, he rang Roger and Harold. It was agreed the five should meet as soon as they could.

"What about my crystal collection Cathy, will you still buy it?" Gillian was still worried about her rent.

"No, but I will give you a job and employ you in my crystal shop; and you can sell your stock through there too. Like you said, I trust you too, I think will get on simply fine. If you are worried about your rent and want to leave that house. I can find you temporary accommodation, you may want a safe place for a while?" Cathy surprised herself with the offer, but it felt just right. She would look at expanding the actual shop into another unit, away from the magic.

The two wives of Martin Bradbury, Bradshaw, Bradgate walked into the solicitors office. They found Martin, Harold and Roger waiting for them with the usual jug of coffee and plate of cakes, these men had a serious cake problem.

"Catherine and Gillian? Please come in and sit down," Harold motioned them into the office. Adam came over and kissed Cathy, and she smiles and whispered to Gillian, "there is a whole life waiting for you after Martin."

145

"As he got a brother," Gillian laughed. It was good to see her smile, she was a totally different woman.

"Well, where do we start, Cathy how much have you told Gillian, no need to go over things twice." Harold took control of the meeting.

"Gillian emailed me to say her husband had gone and emptied her bank account, I do not know how much. We met up and it became obvious she was talking about Martin, so I told her he was my ex-husband. Then I thought it better we all meet up and go from here. Although it does seem that Martin had met Gillian before, he had left me." Cathy brought them up to date.

"I am so sorry," Gillian started.

"Don't be, it isn't our fault we fell for him. But I can assure you, you will get over him quickly!" Cathy smiled at the poor woman.

Harold and Roger filled her in on the details of Martin and Elizabeth. That they had tried to catch him before he had married again, but they were too late.

"We went on a three-week cruise for our honeymoon," Gillian was sad as she told them all. "We spent all the time in the casino and bar, spending as much of my money as he could. It was though he was obsessed with winning a fortune. When we got back, things soon went downhill. He said he was working away many times, as he was a financial consultant. I believed him."

"Oh. I believed he was an accountant too and was investing my money for my own good. Sadly, for him, any money I did have was put back into the online business and stock." Cathy laughed as she remembered his disappointment of her non inheritance. Yes, then he began working away, longer, and longer. I wonder how other people he may have married, and under what name."

"I am Gillian Bradshaw." Gillian began.

"I was Cathy Bradbury and Elizabeth is Bradgate we think." Cathy told her.

Roger coughed, and the two women looked at him. "We think there was at least one other wife, under the name of Bradley. The police are following it up. He is a bit naïve, when he puts his father's name down the same on all the documents."

146

"So, how do we proceed from here," Cathy asked the gents in front of her.

"We will need a statement from Gillian, to add to yours, and your aunt and uncle. Gillian, can I ask how much money he took, or its ok for just the statement?" Adam asked her, sympathy filing his eyes too,

"He cleared out the remains of the sale of my parents' house, about £145,000.00. We had kept it in the joint account as we were looking at buying a property together. I feel so foolish." Gillian was so embarrassed, and at a lost. Her money and future home were gone, and her husband was remarried already.

"Please do not feel you did anything wrong; you are not the first to be scammed by this man. But the more we find out, the longer he will be put away for. So anything you can tell us, the more we build a case."

The group listened to Gillian and took notes, when it was all over, Cathy invited her back to her own cottage in the village, rather than the mill.

"This is my own cottage, you are welcome to stay here, rather than your old place. You will be safe here, I am spending more time at Adams house recently," Cathy smiled at Gillian. She was a slight woman, with the purpliest of red hair she had seen. She looked completely lost.

"Do you want to go and collect some things from your old house, and then stay here and recover from all the shocks. We can take the crystal stock to the mill, there is a spare unit next to mine. We could open a shop to the public, which you could run if you wanted to."

"Why are you being so nice to me?" Gillian wasn't used to people being nice to her, after strict parents and then the husband, why would this woman be nice to her at all.

"Because, I have been, where you are now, and I know it's not a place to be on your own. Lady luck shone on me a few months ago. And I am in a position to be able to help you. We seem to have very same likes and dislikes, tell me, your favourite crystal?" Cathy smiled at her new friend.

"Of course, it has to be amethyst," Gillian said pulling a fabulous amethyst palm stone from her pocket, which looked like it had been rubbed a lot lately.

"Fantastic, I just know we will be wonderful friend Gillian," Cathy told her.

"Can I ask you a question Cathy," Gillian whispered, although only the two of them were in the house.

"Of course, you can," Cathy answered.

"Are you magical? Are you the ghost whisperer that helped the ghosts at the workhouse?" Gillian asked her.

Unsure how to answer, Cathy thought no more secrets. "Yes, I am, my grandmother was Sally Buckley, head of the Circle of the Dove Stone Coven, Green Valley. I did not know anything till about six months ago, when I was mentioned in her will. Does it worry you, Gillian?"

"No, no, not at all, I am a witch too or I was. But I have had to keep it under wraps for so long, my father disapproved of my mother and myself. Part of him providing for us, was we never used magic. I never told Martin, I knew he wouldn't understand, and probably expect me to win the lottery for him. I would love to learn, could you teach me?"

"Ironically, your story is very much like my cousin Elizabeth, her magic was bound as a child as her father was too proud to live with witches. I just didn't know anything until I went to claim my inheritance. Do you want to move in here for a short time, I am not after any rent, just time for you to relax and work out your future. I will help pay your rent on the Upper Valley place, but you are more than welcome here Gillian." Cathy was sincere, her life had turned around, why not help someone else.

"Are you sure," Gillian was uncertain. No one helped her before, and Martin had got rid of any friends she did have.

"100% absolutely. I know he got rid of your friends, he did with mine. When he left me, I only had my Uncle John and that was it. He found me this cottage and helped me move in. Turns out, it was my grandmothers cottage, and it's now mine. Oh Fate, you do work in wonderful ways." Cathy showed Gillian around the small house, "Make yourself at home. Do you want a coffee, or something stronger?"

"Do you have any wine," Gillian asked, "I could do with something other than coffee."

"Just watch this," and Cathy clicked her fingers and two wine glasses and a bottle of chilled white where on the table.

"Wow, was that magic?" Gillian gasped.

"Oh yes you have so much to learn, it is wonderful."

Cathy phoned Adam to update him and said she would stay at the house overnight with Gillian, and she would catch up tomorrow. So, the two exes chatted till the early hours, comparing notes, and toasted to the future together.

Chapter 28

The Ex Is Caught

The next couple of weeks went by in a flash, Cathy had arranged with Harold to rent the "proper" unit near hers at the mill. So, it was transformed into the Crystal Cave. Gillian had moved into the cottage in town, belonging to Cathy and had more or less emptied the tiny house she had shared with her husband. She had boxed up the things he had left, or she felt she didn't want to take with her. The stock of crystals and bits had moved into the shop at the mill. Cathy hadn't yet introduced her to any of the ghosts there, although they secretly had been having a nosey themselves and vetting the new member of the team.

Both Cathy and Gillian were pleased with the new arrangement. Cathy had moved one of the computers into the shop, so they could do some online orders from there. But kept her own unit for the making of hers (and Clara Jane's) jewellery. Clara Jane was happy creating new pieces or works of art she called them, but Gillian was unaware of her. Everyone had thought it best to keep Gillian as normal as possible until after the trial of her current /ex-husband.

Adam rang Cathy to tell her, that they had all the evidence they needed now that they had Gillian's statement to add to Cathy's and her relatives. They had found the four marriage certificates, it appeared there was another woman, living a few towns away, that was also still married to him. He had also preyed on her after her parents had died. Cathy had been the first in a succession of vulnerable women.

The cruise ship was due back in Southampton soon. Elizabeth had been in touch with her parents, for them to visit the following weekend. Adam and his colleagues from the normal police force, thought it would be better to arrest him in Green Valley, rather than Southampton. Let him stay unaware of the situation a while longer. It would help Elizabeth to be parted from him, while at home rather than hundreds of miles away.

Cathy's Aunt and Uncle had been very helpful with the police, both MPA and Normal, (Charles old colleagues.) As much help as they could do and had agreed to let them know as soon as they arrived at the house.

It was agreed that Elizabeth and her husband would go to dinner with Audrey and Charles, on the Saturday evening. Charles had agreed to the house being bugged, so they could record the conversation. The police would be in other rooms in the house just in case. Alf and Eric from the mill, were also on call for any disturbance. The police thought about Cathy being there, as she was family, but decided against it. Cathy and Gillian would be at the police station to greet him after his arrest.

Saturday evening came around very quickly. Everyone was in position as Martin and Elizabeth arrived at her parents' house. Elizabeth was a little worried as she knew she had gone against her parents' wishes. She was already having doubts about Martin, all he had done on the cruise was spend her money. She had looked at her bank account and saw that her investments had a stop on them, so she would ask her parents when she was alone with them.

The old Celica pulled up outside the impressive building, and Elizabeth let herself into her parents' house. Martin followed, surveying the property, and calculating how much it was worth. If he played his cards right with this silly woman, he might actually get enough money to pay off his debts.

Audrey ran to meet her daughter and hugged her close, whilst Charles shook Martin's hand and through tight teeth congratulated him on his wedding. The police had told Charles to play along and not let him become suspicious.

"Oh Elizabeth, welcome home, you look so well, how was the cruise?" Audrey asked her.

Quick to reply, Martin answered for his wife, "Wonderful, we have had a wonderful time." Elizabeth smiled, they had only seen the bars and casino of the cruise for three weeks he spent her money. She felt that her parents knew more than they were saying,

"Something smells good, what's for dinner?" Elizabeth darted into the kitchen, with her mother following. Charles took Martin into the dining room and started to serve the drinks. He wasn't sure what to say, so busied himself, opening a couple of bottles of wine. He knew the police were listening to him, it was strange for this old, retired copper to be on the other side.

Elizabeth and Audrey returned to join them, "Please take your seats, I will bring the starters in, I am afraid it won't be as good as the cruise food."

Elizabeth thought to herself, cruise food, it had been burgers in the casino all the time, the invitation to the captain's table had arrived and he had ripped it up. She never got to wear the fabulous dresses she had bought. It had been casual all the way. She had paid a fortune for a luxury cruise, and she felt so disappointed. He had hardly spoken to her the entire cruise. At night he was too drunk to make the most of the luxurious suite she had booked.

As Audrey brought in the smoked salmon starters, Charles opened the wine. The conversation flowed to where the couple were going to live now, they were married.

In open cheek, Martin actually suggested that Audrey and Charlie move into Elizabeth's annex, and the two of them could move into the bigger house, ready for their offspring. He would do his work from the office upstairs, so he was on hand to help out.

"Remind me, what business are you in?" Audrey asked meekly, playing the part so well.

"I am a financial accountant, I work from home, but travel the country as well. So, it makes sense we live next to you, so Elizabeth has help with the children. I help people with their investments, making the best deal for people. Maybe I could have a look at yours one day Charlie, and get you a better deal." Martin, chest out, full of importance.

The man was full of himself, Charles stopped the spluttering he was about to do by pretending he has a tickle in his throat.

Elizabeth thought to herself, it takes action to get children, they had not actually consummated their marriage yet.

Audrey sat and watched the four times married man, and wished she had her witch powers back to turn him into a frog,

"I already have a financial adviser, Martin," Charles replied, "Everything is in good hands,"

"Oh, I am your son in law now, Charlie," Martin quietly began to fume, this idiot may just be harder than he had imagined. "It is my duty to make sure my wife is well taken care of, and that includes going over your finances too."

"I don't think so, young man. You may have taken my daughter off to marry her, but my finances will remain exactly where I can see them. I will add that your last visit wasn't the pleasantest of visits. You mentioned a lot of names in this house, and about other people's inheritance."

"Oh, rubbish old man," Martin was getting out of his depth. How much had he said before about the cousin, and her non-existent inheritance. He had drunk far too much wine, and didn't quite remember.

"Anyone want any more wine, I will get the next course, Elizabeth, will you help me?" Audrey tried to change the conversation. She had noticed Elizabeth was incredibly quiet, and not at all sunburnt from three weeks in the Mediterranean.

The two ladies went into the kitchen, and overheard Martin begin to have a dig at Charles.

"Oh Mum, what have I done?" Elizabeth tried to hold back the tears, "I am so, so sorry."

"Worry not sweet girl, everything will be sorted out soon. I promise," her mother held her close.

"You know something don't you, you are the one that put a stop on my bank aren't you?" Elizabeth was now waking up to the fact the situation she was in most be serious if her parents had done that.

"Here, takes this casserole into the dining room, before those two-start fighting. I promise it will be alright soon, and we will be here for you." Her mother passed the food over as they walked back to the dining room.

Elizabeth wondered what on earth was going to happen next. She soon found out as they walked into the dining room. Martin had hold of her father with his arm twisted behind his back.

"What is going on here?" she demanded,

"The old fool says he isn't giving this house to us, and that I won't get any of his money," Martin was sweating now, as he had been caught out by his latest wife.

"I think I should call the POLICE" shouted Charles, his arm feeling like it might break. "This is assault in my own home."

"Shut up you stupid old man, you have no idea what you are talking about. Your daughter said everything was in her name, so she has her husband now, and it is all mine." An evil laugh escaped from Martin as he threatened Charles.

As he was laughing, the dining room door suddenly opened, and so did the patio doors, which had been left unlocked on purpose.

Adam led the rest of the arrest team into the room. Audrey pulled Elizabeth near to her, and Martin let go of Charles.

"Martin Bradbury, also known as Martin Bradshaw, Martin Bradley and Martin /Bradgate?" Then the officer uttered the magic words, "You are under arrest. You will be booked, processed, and depending on the charges allowed to make bail or be released on your own recognizance, or for more serious charges, you will be arraigned where you will either be allowed to make bail or be remanded."

"What the hell are you talking about?" Martin was suddenly beginning to look worried, had his bitch of a first wife split on him? Did she really have CCTV of the day at her crummy shop?"

Adam continued, "You are being arrested for various offences, starting with assaulting Mr Jones in his own home. Assaulting your first wife Catherine Collins in her own shop. For being a bigamist, at current count you have three consecutive wives. For defrauding various establishments and finally for embezzlement of various investment fund, whilst appearing to be a registered financial adviser. Cuff him lads and take him to the station."

Martin tried to make a run for it, But Alf and Eric were already in his way, and he ran right into them, "Oh not you to again," he sighed.

"Afraid so mate," Eric laughed, and handed him to the police to take away. After the commotion had calmed down, Adam explained all to Elizabeth, she cried, then she laughed with relief. She hugged her parents and asked what will happen next.

"One of the first things to happen, my dear Elizabeth and Audrey, is that Catherine is going to unbind your magical powers and train you both. I have held you both back so long, I was so

154

proud, I didn't want anything magical to spoil my career. I never realised what I had done until I met your cousin Catherine." Charles held his wife and daughter and tears poured down all their faces.

"Magic?" Elizabeth exclaimed, and then fainted.

"Put her to bed and let her rest," Adam told them, "When she is ready to meet Cathy, as a friend and cousin, she will be waiting. I best get to the station before Cathy and Gillian rip the poor man's head off. Tell her, she is in excellent company of being duped by this man, Goodnight."

With that, Elizabeth was put on the sofa, and the trio was left alone.

Back at the station, Cathy and Gillian were all dressed up in the similar casual outfits and waited for the arrival of Martin. Adam had warned them to not jeopardise the case, and they both agreed they would just stand there as he was signed into his cell.

Martin was fighting all the way to the station, and pleading his innocence, as he walked through the door, his eye caught sight of Cathy and Gillian, and he knew then he had no chance to plead innocent, He had made a total mess of everything.

Duly signed in and rights read to him, Martin Bradbury, his original surname was put into a cell, all his possessions were confiscated. His one phone call was to his solicitor, who wasn't very happy to hear from him at all. The two ex-wives left the building, smiling.

155

Chapter 29

Celebration Dinner

The boardroom at the mill was abuzz with everyone. Cynthia had wanted to have a party to celebrate Clara Jane staying, but no one had really wanted a party. But now the original party idea, had turned into a massive celebration, Wendy and Kim had done their usual magnificent buffet, and the wine was flowing freely.

Gillian had taken on a lease to rent Cathy's cottage in the village. The crystal shop had taken off so well, that it kept her busy. She hadn't flinched when introduced to the ghosts of the mill. She had even found her own familiar, a delightful whippet dog, named Marley, who also got on very well with Oskar and Hamish. She had also heard from the detectives, that Martin had still got her inheritance in his bank account, so she was hopeful to get some or even all of it back in her bank.

Clara Jane flitted from the workroom to the shop, through the walls, and everyone just smiled. The young ghost, from 1883 had finally got her childhood back. Although, she still was not allowed in the Temple Room, without Cathy.

Audrey and Elizabeth were never away from the mill. Elizabeth even took a tenancy of one of the mill cottages. Sshe had decided she needed her own independence after all this time. She too hoped that she would get some of the £30,000 back that she had spent with Martin, but she still had the rest of the money from the house sale. She was happy again with her life and was looking at a part time job in the mill office. She thought that with Cathy and Gillian, they would made a good trio of the now ex-wives. She felt free, freer that she had ever known. So, she chatted away, like the newfound woman she was turning into.

Elizabeth and Gillian soon found themselves stood next to David and Nigel the archaeology brothers. They smiled to each other, knowingly, and they both wondered what their futures would hold. They were both now witches in training, and their same ex-husband, was serving at least 15 years in prison for bigamy, theft, and threatening behaviour.

Cathy and Adam were planning on going back to the log cabin, with no phone signals, for a few days longer this time.

Sally was busy running "How to be a Witch" lessons to Audrey, Elizabeth, and Gillian. She had been reunited with her daughter and granddaughter, who were so grateful to Catherine for how she had got Sally back for them. They had a lot of lost time to make with Sally, too, just like Cathy had.

Harold, John, Roger, and Stephen were huddled in the corner, near the wine table, they had had enough excitement for a while. Although Harold was keeping his eye on Sally, he was so grateful to Cathy, who had got her back for him now.

All the members of the Coven were gathered in the room together, when Cynthia made an announcement that shocked them all.

"Ladies and Gentlemen, Please can I have your attention. Some of the older members of the Circle of the Dove Stone Coven, feel that our time has come to pass on our places at the table to the younger members of the Coven. With Catherine taking her rightful place at the head of said Coven. There are a few relatives of ours that are now ready to take over the reins, with our help of course. We already have three new members being trained by Sally. Pat and Regina both have granddaughters, Becki and Inese, that are willing to step up to the take their place in the Coven. Pat, Edith, Margaret, and Desdemona, and I will be on call if you need anything. There will have a transition period, with the new members learning the way of the Coven. Thank you, Catherine, on behalf of everyone, but we do have a new quest for you though."

"What will that be Cynthia," asked a speechless Cathy, she never thought of anyone new in the Coven, least of all being led by herself.

"We want you to find Desdemona's granddaughter, Donna Maria. When you do, we hope she will join you, with the other young members of the Circle of the Dove Stone Coven" Cynthia smiled at Cathy, "We know you will do it."

Cathy stood in the middle of the crowd of witches, wizards, werewolves and even people. like Uncle John and Uncle Charles.

How did she deserve to be surrounded by such marvellous people in her life now.

Adam took her hand and held her close as everyone raised a glass to the wonderful Catherine, granddaughter of Sally Buckley. The new leader of the Circle of the Dove Stone Coven.

"Gran," Cathy whispered to Sally, "Can you teach me how to shapeshift into a bird, so I can fly the valley with Adam sometime?"

"One day at a time, sweet Catherine," her grandmother smiled sadly, "But yes, you will be able to do just that soon. But we need to be careful, something I have never told you. Your mother learnt to shapeshift because of your father. They were roaming the Swiss Alps in the shape of red deer when they were shot by a hunter. So, one day at a time, my dear, please.

"So, that means that Uncle John is .... "Cathy continued. "Oh dear, not tonight," her grandmother pleased gently.

Adam leaned over her and gave her a big kiss in front of everyone and the crowd cheered.

"Let's all celebrate and raise a toast to Cathy, the woman that has saved the enchanted mill, and here's to many more quests." He laughed, holding her tight.

"Here, here," the crowd clinked their glasses, and cheered Cathy as the Coven Leader, "to the next adventure!"

Alf and Eric appeared, with two of the tiniest gorgeous slim women, Cathy had seen. "Can we introduce you to our wives, Rimmon and Rowan," Alf said to Cathy. "When the dust settles, would you both come to dinner, at our house. It is high on the hills, a distance away, as you can appreciate with us being giants?"

"Thank you, that will be amazing, thank you, and it is so nice to meet you both." Cathy replied, all these new friends she was making, genuine friends too.

"Cathy," laughed Peter, the archaeologist, "about your next adventure, I have a site I would love you to visit with me."

"Not tonight," his wife laughed, leading him away, "Tonight is Cathy's celebration."

Cathy wandered over to her Uncle John, Roger, and Sally, smiling sweetly, she whispered to them all, "So, now that Clara

Jane is reunited and my ex is serving his time, just exactly how much am I worth now?"

The three of them all laughed loud together, causing everyone else to look round at them.

"Shall I tell her, or you Sally?" laughed Uncle John.

"Oh, darling Catherine," Sally then leaned forward and whispered in her hear, "give or take a bit, a couple of mansions here and there, I would say around twenty million, with restrictions, of course!"

"Wow, that's a lot of money." she grinned, and while she was on a roll she asked, "So may I ask another question, what is in the cellar?"

"Never you mind, not a story for now. Maybe another day, but we can assure you it is nothing to worry about." The three of them laughed, along with Adam.

"One day, I am sure you will tell me," Cathy and her friends all laughed together.

"One day you will have to know." Sally replied.

To be continued…

159

Printed by BoD™in Norderstedt, Germany

9 781915 889287